WITTERKIN

W.K. GREYLING

Paperback ISBN: 978-1-7775489-7-1

Edited by Allister Thompson

First edition: May 2022

www.wkgreyling.com

CONTENTS

PROLOGUE

Living wild species are like a library of books still unread. Our heedless destruction of them is akin to burning the library without ever having read its books.
—John Dingell

History is nothing but assisted and recorded memory.
-George Santayana

The being sang as she took in the world around her—the sun, shining through gauzy clouds, the small blue bird chirping on the nearby fence, the distant patter of human footsteps in the field beyond. She had recorded such sights and sounds for millennia. Each hung suspended inside her, like a bright star in a vast universe.

Her nearby kin sang along with her, their voices melding to create one perfect sound. She sensed their peace, but not their observations—these would be shared after nightfall, while the world slept.

The bird flew away, and humans holding shiny buckets approached a gap in the fence. Their bodies were covered, from head to foot, in bulky material. Her memories told her this was unusual. On hot days, humans always showed skin. What could this signify?

The ragged opening in the fence was yet another anomaly. The fence had been carefully maintained for the past one hundred and fourteen years and fifty-three days. Then, just yesterday, humans tore down a section of it. If she could understand their language, then she might learn their intent, but in her recorded memory, no human had ever tried to teach her.

The human at the front stood still for a few moments, eyes narrowed, then he held the bucket over one of her kin. As he tipped it, a dark liquid spilled out…

PART ONE:

THE WINDSINGER

CHAPTER ONE

The rhythmic tapping of a chisel echoed in the stone workshop. Other sounds faded beneath it until Nya Stary imagined she was in a copse of trees listening to a woodpecker in some far-off branch.

The chisel paused, and voices slipped back in. The trees vanished.

She suppressed a sigh and looked sideways at her older brother, who stood by her listening to a young man at a desk explain how wind passing through a gap in a memorial stone could be made to sound like their dead father.

The man at the desk was the town Windsinger, Yaromir Korobin. Yaro for short. His workshop was an open room at least sixty feet long. The desk near the door served to divide the space, creating an area for customers while still allowing them to glimpse the cluttered workshop beyond.

The chisel started up again, and Nya's hands unclenched a little.

She and her brother, Goran, had already attended the ceremonial burning of their father's body. The stone was last and most important. But first, the gap in its center had to be cut just so, like the narrow opening in the mouthpiece of a funerary flute.

Wind whistled through windows because of such gaps. *Don't let the dead in,* people said on windy days, and they stuffed damp rags into windowpanes and doorframes to make the sound stop. But Windsinger Yaro created such gaps, fearlessly and precisely, in the centers of memorial stones. Nya had heard him explain how it was done many times before. She knew it all as well as she knew the soft, deep tones of his voice, his large hazel eyes and chiseled cheekbones, brown hair that was always unruly, as if he had just come down from the cemetery on the hill, shaken by the sea breeze; he wore a long apron when working, and his well-muscled hands were always powdered by stone dust. As he spoke, a bead of sweat trickled down his temple, creating a darker streak through the dust.

She sighed and shook her head. She was distracting herself, trying not to think about whose memorial stone they were ordering and how he had died.

Nya had never been close to her father. His first wife had left him when Goran was only three. His second wife—Nya's mother—had died in a carriage accident when Nya was fourteen. Afterward, her father had barricaded himself in his study, drinking himself to death over the course of several years. Nya had witnessed the terrible decline, powerless to stop it.

She regarded her brother thoughtfully. He was normally jovial and well kept. Now his clothes were in disarray, and shadows darkened his eyes. She should not leave him alone this night.

"Nya?" Yaro said.

She jumped at the sound of her name.

The Windsinger's voice softened. "What do you think?"

Her eyes flicked up to his, snagged for the briefest moment, like dust in a bird's wing, before falling again. Her answer came out in little more than a whisper. "I think you know exactly how he should sound and where to put his stone."

After a brief pause, Goran asked Yaro a question about the stone's height, and the drone of voices went on.

Nya waited for the comforting tap of the chisel, but it had gone silent at the sound of her name. She craned her head, peering past piles of unworked windstone toward the far end of the workshop. At last, she spotted the young chiseler, who stood frozen like a rabbit caught in an eagle's stare. Her mouth thinned in irritation. He was probably terrified to see her there.

Many of the townsfolk suspected Nya of being a witch. Of course, she was not. She simply gathered herbs and made medicines, but there was no way to prove them wrong. Her goblin-like looks didn't help matters. She had huge hazel eyes, a small nose and mouth, and dogteeth that jutted out, rendering her smile more feral than friendly. Her brown hair was straight as a pin, and her body was just as pin-like. And at twenty-one years of age, things weren't going to get better.

On a whim, she lifted her hand behind her back and traced a random shape with her finger in the air. Her head tilted toward the boy again, who had gone as white as the windstone he had been working on. All of a sudden, he dropped the chisel. The metal clang cracked through the space, silencing Yaro's voice.

Nya pressed her lips together to keep from grinning. She shouldn't be. What kind of horrible person enjoyed teasing a frightened boy while choosing her father's windstone? Her cheeks heated, and she looked away.

Her brother turned at the sound of the dropped tool, and Nya innocently followed his gaze. The boy scrambled for the chisel with a mumbled apology and turned away from them both.

"That kid doesn't do the actual work, does he?" Goran asked. "I mean, make the slit and all."

Nya winced at the question. She risked a glance at Yaro, but he didn't appear offended by Goran's ignorance and lack of manners. Perhaps he had been asked the question before. It wouldn't have surprised her. Folk would want to be sure that the master and not his helper had crafted their relative's expensive stone.

Yaro replied, "No, he only does the rough work. The facing and such. I finish the stones." He paused, looking back at the workshop as if seeing it for the first time. "I suppose I'll have to train someone to do what I do someday. No one lives forever." With a sigh, he got up from his chair and ran a callused hand down a giant piece of parchment hanging on the wall. A detailed sketch of the cemetery spread over it, the center parts faded with age. The diagram was ancient. Generations of Windsingers had added to it over the years. Yaro's fingers trailed along a freshly inked area in the bottom half of the page. "Here. This is the percussion area. The grunters and chucklers go here, and some sighers on the edge. I'll take you up there in a few days, when the wind is strong."

Nya stared at the small, inked area, remembering her father's dry chuckle. She had not heard it for years, but Yaro knew how he had sounded before sorrow set in.

As if he had been listening to her thoughts, Yaro cleared his throat and mimicked her father's old chuckle. "Is that it?"

Nya's eyes pricked with tears. "That's it. That's him."

"That'll do," Goran agreed.

They left Yaro in the workshop and climbed into the waiting carriage outside, Nya lifting her town skirts to avoid crushing them in the door. Goran's waiting sweetheart, Faina, loosed a worried coo as Goran settled in beside her. She was slender and blond, with wide-set eyes and a delicate chin. Truth be told, she looked more like Goran than Nya did.

"I'm fine," he grunted, squaring his shoulders. As the carriage started moving, he looked pointedly at Nya. "What is it between you two?"

"Between me and who?"

"You know who. Don't play dumb."

She shook her head and looked out the dusty carriage window toward the bay. "There's nothing between me and Yaro."

"You used to seek him out at dances," Goran said.

That had been back when her mother was still alive. Back when folks had paid Nya as much mind as they would a mouse running on the docks.

Faina chirped in agreement. "You two were always in some corner, talking."

Nya turned from the window to face them. "I was only a girl then, and he was the only young person besides me who never danced."

Goran chuckled. "Poor Yaro. Pa used to say that you two were like peas in a pod."

"Why?" Nya asked, genuinely curious about something she had not heard before, but Faina flashed him a warning glance, and he went silent.

Nya shook her head at them both. Yaro was good-looking and respected. Everything she was not. Why anyone would lump them together was a mystery to her.

A blessed silence fell, and she returned to the scene outside the window.

The ocean was steel gray that morning, its surface blending with the overcast sky. Boats floated here and there, sails down and nets out. The town of Sundyr stretched around the bay in a chaotic jumble of docks, warehouses, pubs, and as the roads climbed up away from the water, stone houses with thatched roofs and unshuttered windows. Yaro's workshop lay near the edge of Cemetery Hill, a huge finger of grassy land that loomed over Sundyr, blocking the early-morning rays.

The clopping of horses grew more labored as the road steepened. A man walking by with his donkey slowed and stared at Nya, then lifted a bony hand to make a warding sign. Nya winked at him, and he scowled. Sighing, she pulled the curtain across the window and slumped into her seat.

She didn't open it again until the ground plateaued, and the bumpy cobbles changed into firm, beaten earth, letting her know she had left the town proper. She smiled faintly at the swaying wheat fields. The mountains, distant yet, were a familiar purple line on the horizon. Her eyes lingered on them, not seeing the bare stone anymore but something green and ethereal, a touch of magic that gathered in a ring at their base.

The Witterkin.

Something strange had happened the last time she visited them.

She had approached them slowly, stooping to pick rare weeds and slip them into her belt pouch. The Witterkin seemed to attract odd plants. And maybe odd people too.

They were unlike anything she'd ever seen. If she was even *seeing* them. From a distance, they looked like a two-foot-high green haze resting on the rocky foot of the mountain, but as she drew closer, they grew denser and more mysterious. Vague lines became apparent, indicating that the haze contained separate parts. Separate entities. Pale, lightning-shaped stems flickered deep in their cores. Neither wind nor insects disturbed the Witterkin, and they cast no shadow.

These facts alone rendered them bizarre and unsettling. But what truly stunned Nya was the sound they made—an unearthly sigh that held within it a thousand distant, distorted voices.

They had rested at the mountain's foot from time immemorial. Unchanging and unchanged.

The townfolk's feelings about them had certainly changed over the years. Folks used to worship them, but as centuries passed and new beliefs swept in from other lands, altars to them were forsaken and finally taken down. The Witterkin were still held by many to be sacred, but those who visited them did so for less arcane reasons. Since the

Witterkin were exclusive to Sundyr, people came from distant lands to study them from state-owned viewing areas.

Most Witterkin, however, still rested on private property. By law, the landowners had to maintain a sturdy wooden fence around them. In addition, a city watchman was tasked with walking the entire length of the Witterkin fence—a three-day journey around the mountains—every six months to ensure there were no violations. Animals usually stayed clear of the Witterkin, but there were cases of people committing suicide by jumping from the fence into them. Falling full-body into the Witterkin was like leaping into fire. If the jumper was not rescued quickly enough, he would die.

Nya's own grandmother had been dragged out of them alive when she was still a young woman. Since she had been a stranger to Sundyr and unable to recall her former life, the incident had roused suspicion. Old tales spoke of the Witterkin as a gateway to "the land of the Good Folk," one that let elves and monsters through. Given her strange looks and convenient amnesia, many had suspected Nya's grandmother to be one of them.

Nya snorted. She was probably just another sightseer who, for whatever reason, had decided to escape her life.

Thoughts about her dead gram kept Nya so distracted that she hadn't noticed the change in the Witterkin until she was almost at the fence.

It had been late afternoon, and the air seemed heavy and full of molten light. A hawk circling overhead let out a keening cry, as if in warning to the world below. Nya lifted her eyes from a plant she was tucking into her belt pouch and tilted her head. The cry should have melted into the high-pitched sighing of the Witterkin. But it did not, because their sound had changed. It was lower, and though she couldn't put her finger on how, it sounded menacing.

She grasped hold of the fence to steady herself. What was wrong with these Witterkin? Or was anything wrong? Maybe the sound lowered periodically. How would anyone know what the Witterkin sounded like a hundred years ago? Or a thousand?

She loosened her steel grip on the fence rail. Should she tell someone?

Best not to. If she were the first to report it, and it became a serious issue, then her name would be forever tied to it, like a curse. Knowing her luck, they would probably blame it on her. Say that she had poisoned the Witterkin with her potions.

She went still, listening, and then drew slowly back. Smoothing the raised hairs on her arms, she returned home.

Later that day, her father died, and she came to view the Witterkin's menacing sound as a portent rather than as a problem.

But now...

Her brows tugged together in a little frown. Her father's death had been a tragedy...for *her and Goran*. A kind man had died and left them orphaned. For a day or two, the sun had dimmed, and the birds had wailed at the calamity.

Except that they had not. The birds had not mourned, the sun had not darkened, and the Witterkin had not pronounced her father's death. Something else was happening to the Witterkin. The marked change in tone could be harmless, or it might indicate a deeper problem.

Either way, she had been right to keep it to herself. If the change extended to the viewing areas, the sheriff would know about it anyway.

The carriage turned off the main road and started down another.

The wide, flat land that lay between Sundyr and the mountains had soil so rich and dark that seeds sprouted just from smelling it—or at least, that's what folk liked to say. In reality, farming was backbreaking work, and her grandfather had not been the first landowner to quit and rent out portions to tenant farmers. The decision had broken up the land's green blanket into a patchwork quilt. Nya eyed one small patch on her father's property. The tiny cottage that accompanied it was newly vacant. She should tell Goran she wanted it. After all, he would marry soon and have children, and how well would she fit in to that household?

The cottage had a good unshaded area for planting, and a south-facing window. She wouldn't mind living there.

Sorrow welled in her as she thought about her little space back at the manor, her life before her mother's death.

Her fingers had memorized the feel of a delicate vine her mother had carved into the banister—one of many marks Aldona had left on the house.

And she left me to go on too.

It was true. Her mother would not have put up with Nya's moping. She would have told her to sit straight and proud, because she was no brown mouse.

Well, at least that part of it was true. She was more of a brown spider now.

***

Late that evening, the family lawyer arrived to discuss Adrion's will with Goran. Nya, buried deep in one of her grandmother's tomes, didn't hear him enter and was surprised when the maid tapped on her door to say she was wanted in the study.

The manor was shadowy with candlelight. The house was small in comparison with others in the area outside the town proper. The first floor held the kitchen and dining hall, a spacious sitting room, and her father's study, the second, seven well-appointed bedrooms of various sizes, most never used. The few household servants lived on the top floor.

Nya traced the vine along the banister as she descended the stairs. She would not weep at the prospect of leaving. What good were these stone walls to her? This bit of wood under her hand? She refused to linger in this house like an unwelcome phantom, frightening guests away with her presence. Goran and Faina deserved better.

She pushed open the study's heavy door, crossed to her father's old marble-topped table, and dropped into a vacant seat beside her brother. A hint of pipe smoke and sandalwood lingered in the air, reminding her of her father. She drew a tight breath and tried for a smile. It did not happen. Her top lip merely tugged up, baring her jutting dogteeth to the lamplight.

The lawyer, a stout, bearded man with a receding hairline, nodded to her across the table before returning his attention to the tidy sheets of paper in front of him. "Thanks for joining us, Nya. I won't take much of your time." He cleared his throat and blinked several times. "To put it plainly, your father made the unusual decision of splitting his estate between his son and daughter. He left it to Goran to decide which bits you would get. In order to make this decision, your brother had to know the worth of every asset and acre. Fortunately for us, Adrion was a meticulous man." He lifted his hands over the sheets. "It's all here. So we've sorted it out in less than an hour."

Nya did not move. Her eyes flicked to Goran's, but her brother's face was inscrutable. She swallowed dryly. "Go on."

The lawyer selected a large sheet from the stack and passed it to her. "This is a map of your father's property. The red line marks the new boundary between Goran's land and yours."

Nya ran her finger over the irregular line. The southern half of the property contained the manor and a handful of tenant farms. The northern half was larger, stretching into the foot of the nearby mountain, and while it contained fewer tenant farms, they were well established and more productive than their southern neighbors. She pushed a fist against her mouth to hide a quivering smile. She hadn't expected to get a quarter of the Stary property, never mind half. Her father had truly loved her. The thought made her eyes prick with tears. "So," she cleared her throat and blinked her eyes dry, "I'm to get the land at the mountain and Goran's to get the manor."

Her brother touched the corner of the page. His voice sounded odd when he spoke, distant and soft like he was reciting poetry. "No. It's the other way around, actually. You're to get the manor, and I'm to get the mountain."

She loosed a soft snort. "Good one. That almost made me laugh."

"I'm serious."

"No, you're not. You can't be. You'll marry soon and—"

"And I plan to build a new house by the mountain. It won't be as well appointed, not at first, but in time..."

Her smile froze in place. She stared sightlessly at the red line, her head beginning to throb.

Goran was still talking. "Father left you enough to keep this place running. And you—"

"No." She dropped her hand on the table. "Stop this, Goran. I know you feel sorry for me, but I don't need or want you to fall on your sword. I would have been happy with a little cottage and some coin to keep me going. This house... It's yours, and people know it. So let me have the land at the mountain and be done with it."

In the silence that followed, the lawyer leaned in and passed Nya another page, this one with a signature on it. "This is the deed to your property, Nya. I called you down to give it to you, not to ask if you wanted it. You can sell the property to another member of your direct family—that being your brother—but you can't give it away. The will stipulates that the estate and all its contents..."

His reedy voice droned on. Nya's dark hair fell over the jagged foot of the mountain. A vague thought tickled the back of her mind, telling her something was wrong, but she couldn't focus on it. The room seemed too bright.

She felt her brother's hand on her shoulder.

"You'll do well," he whispered. "Having the house will mean going into town more. Meeting people. That's one of the reasons I chose to do this."

She opened her mouth, and then closed it. Goran still believed that thrusting herself into folk's faces would make them accept her. But it didn't work that way. Evidently, her brother understood people as well as he understood her—not at all.

The thought pressed painfully on her sore heart. She lurched to her feet, mumbled a thank-you to the lawyer, then grabbed a bottle of brandy off the table and stormed out of the room.

Hours later, she lay awake in the darkness, her head spinning from the drink as she tried to make sense of what had happened. Did Goran hate this house? Was there a secret he had kept from her, one so dark that he wanted nothing better than to remove himself from the property? If she'd gotten to know him better growing up, perhaps he would have confided in her.

Too late. She was no more than a game piece to him now. Something to be moved across a board. He had decided *for* her, without asking her opinion, and now he was moving on with his life and his plans. *Too late, too late, too late.*

She closed her eyes and tried to stop the spinning. A gust of wind rattled the window, and raindrops pattered against the glass. Like a sleepwalker, she rose out of bed and crossed to the window. Her fingers found the old, twisted length of cloth wedged into one side and peeled it away. She stood, listening, waiting for the dead to speak, whisper a secret to the darkness.

But the wind did not return.

CHAPTER TWO

The next day was bright and dry, but Nya was not free to enjoy it until Goran had schooled her on what she was to do on a daily, weekly, monthly, and yearly basis in order to keep the estate running smoothly—tasks that he and Father had once shared. She listened dutifully while her head throbbed, and her bleary eyes struggled to focus. Goran had no mercy for her, and was even a little impatient, as if he couldn't wait to escape his duties. Maybe his choice to abandon the house was as simple as that: escape. Maybe he even thought she would do a better job at running the place than he would, once she was trained.

Maybe, maybe.

By noon, her headache had eased, and clasping her foraging pouch to her waist, she took the sloping path that led up to the Witterkin. She wanted to investigate the odd sound. And besides, it always felt good to bury herself and all her small problems in the green face of eternity. She had been going there for years and would continue to, she promised herself, no matter whose land the Witterkin sat on.

This time, she heard it from a distance—the deeper, menacing tone. It reminded her, in some primal way, of a warning bell. But warnings were given for a reason, so that others could heed them. Who was meant to heed this warning? She approached the fence warily and closed her hands around the wooden rail.

I am not afraid, she thought as the sound filled her, and the flickering green depths leaned in like a starry sky.

She drew back slowly, a minute or an hour later, her head fuzzy, trembling as if she had nearly fallen. She had never lost herself so thoroughly in the Witterkin. But despite her efforts to understand what was happening, she had no answers. Nothing unusual stirred in the Witterkin's green depths, or at least nothing that she—a mere mortal—could detect. She turned away reluctantly and wandered for a while, still dazed, through the waving grass and field weeds. She'd planned to walk the fence to the next property over, see how far the change in tone extended, but she no longer felt up to it. *Tomorrow,* she thought.

As she headed south, her eyes chanced upon a yellow-leafed plant she didn't recognize. In a few quick movements, it was out of the ground and folded into her belt pouch. She would examine it as soon as she got home.

She spied Goran from a distance. He trotted on horseback up a narrow road toward the foot of the mountain.

Three of his friends trailed close behind, followed by a horse-drawn wagon that showed signs of being heavily laden. So. He wasn't wasting any time building his new house. She wondered if he would start sleeping out there too.

Be happy for him. If this was what he truly wanted, why object to it? It was no use anyway. The deed was signed. Done was done.

"Done as dinner," she muttered as she swung open the door to her herb shed. As was her habit, she paused at the entrance and drank in a potent breath of dried plants, searching for a hint of mildew. Once, she had been unaware of a small leak in the roof, and two bundles of lungwort had been ruined. The plants weren't always easy to find, and they took time to dry.

The shed was attached to an old storage room next to the kitchen. Light streamed unhindered through its three tall windows. Every inch of the remaining three walls were covered by hanging plants.

Satisfied that nothing was amiss, she sank down at a workbench in the center of the room and spread one of the yellow leaves over a slab of white marble. She studied it for a moment or two with a magnifying glass before opening her grandmother's tome and gently turning the pages. Vivid paintings of plants, complete with instructions on their use, filled the yellowed paper. And a couple of mysterious diagrams too. A year ago, when Nya still had a bustling business, a nosy girl had spied one of the diagrams and shrank back against her mother, mumbling something about witchcraft. Her mother had taken one look at the page and fled. After that... Well, Nya still had a few nervous, desperate customers, but most stayed well away from her and what they had started to call her "lair."

"Doesn't matter," she muttered. If they needed herbs, there was a perfectly good apothecary in town. Of course, he did not have Nya's catalogue. She had added a few extra sheets to the book, and over the years her own discoveries had spread over the pages, much as Yaro added to his family's map of memorial stones.

"Yaro," she whispered, wanting to feel the pleasure and bitterness that name evoked before banishing it from her mind. She hadn't lied to Goran and Faina about her relationship with Yaro. There was nothing between them now. Only the awkwardness of shared memories.

She closed the book with a faint smile. As she had suspected, the yellow-leafed plant was not there. Time to experiment. Using a razor blade, she cut off a small section of the leaf and lifted it to her temple. She held it there for some moments, eyes squeezed shut. Sometimes, she thought she could sense the purpose of a plant just by "listening" to it. It was a silly idea, but she had been right so often that she couldn't set it aside. After a long silence, she yawned and blinked. Nothing. She popped the leaf into her mouth.

Most plants were not poisonous to humans, but if anything went awry, she was confident her grandmother's purge would resolve the problem. She always kept a flask of it on the bench, just in case.

The plant had very little taste. Which again was good.

A soft knock fell on the door. "Nya? It's Yasna."

Nya grinned at the older woman's voice. Yasna was the closest thing to a friend she had, and she could do with one now, though the timing was not great. She liked to spend some minutes alone after eating strange plants. If she had to make an emergency purge, she didn't want to have to explain why.

She tossed a cloth over the yellow leaf and rushed to the door. Yasna's full lips parted in a smile, revealing startlingly white teeth. She was an energetic woman of sixty years with tightly curling gray hair and a shiny button nose. Her father had been a wealthy ship captain, and like many men who spent much of their time at sea, he had taken a foreign mistress and settled with her on some distant island. When the woman died, he brought his young daughter back to Sundyr to be raised by a nursemaid. The captain drowned soon after in a storm, leaving young Yasna an orphan, and one who did not look like she fit in to the seaside town. Her skin was the rich color of peeled chestnuts, and she liked to polish it with almond oil.

She had lived in Sundyr long enough to be accepted, though perhaps not embraced. At least, Nya thought wryly, folk didn't make warding signs when they saw her.

"You're looking a bit pink, Nitty," Yasna commented, her smile faltering. Her button nose lifted, and she sniffed at Nya's face. "You haven't been drinking, have you?"

"Of course not." She meant to wink but didn't quite manage it. Her eyes felt oddly heavy. She wriggled her toes, wondering at the tingles in them. Had she been sitting too long?

Suddenly, a crushing wave of dizziness rolled over her. She grabbed at the door to keep from falling. "I need…" She threw a desperate glance at the bench, then her legs gave way and she knew no more.

***

Nya opened her eyes and stared at the ceiling of her bedchamber.

She should be ashamed. Call herself every foolish name she could think of. Instead, she bit her lip to keep from grinning wildly. She had finally done it. After years of searching, she had happened on something truly valuable. How many uses might the plant have? Could it be made into a sleeping draft? Numb skin if used topically? So many possibilities…

She sat up with caution, relieved that the world didn't spin. "How long have I been out?" she asked the shadow in the corner.

Yasna started and then rushed to Nya's side, her white skirts whooshing against her skinny legs. "A few hours. I couldn't find your brother, so I had the servants carry you upstairs. The doctor came and went. Said that whatever you ate will probably wear off, but if anything changes, I should call for him again."

It seemed that the doctor had divined what happened. Nya hoped that wouldn't come back to bite her in the future. She offered a tight nod. "Thank you, Yasna. It was kind of you to fetch him." She drew off the blanket and swung out of bed. A heaviness in her limbs told her that the plant's effects hadn't completely worn off. She took three steady steps toward the door.

"Nitty—"

"I'm quite well. Does Lucky need another flea bath?"

"Well, yes, but—"

"Then let's go."

A half hour later, she stepped out of Yasna's small buggy and followed her through a gate and up a cobblestone path.

Yasna led a simple life. Her only servant, an old sailor who endlessly twisted his beard when his hands weren't occupied, hobbled up the walkway ahead of them, waving chickens aside with a crooked cane. The stone house was more of a cottage than a manor. Its upper floor had only two bedchambers. The roof was of thatch rather than clay or slate, and the grounds were bare of hedges and other niceties. A vine with leaves the size of human heads crept over a front window. Every time Nya came by, it was higher. She resisted the urge to tear it off as she went inside.

"If you won't take coin, then let me braid your hair," Yasna offered some time later. Nya sat in a chair by the woodstove, picking through the cat's orange fur in search of flea eggs. Yasna stood behind her, occasionally stirring a pot of boiling water and stavesacre seed. A plate of cookies and hot, sweet tea sat on a short table nearby. "It's what I always did for my ma," Yasna went on. "You'd look fine with braids."

"I'd look like an ugly spider. More than I already do."

"You're not ugly, Nitty. You're striking." She tugged gently on Nya's hair, nails clicking as she braided. The sound was oddly calming.

Nya's eyes closed, and she let Lucky wriggle away. "Sure, if you mean that people feel struck after seeing me."

Yasna did not reply. The wind answered for her, a tapping of vine leaves against glass. Yaro loved the wind, Nya thought sleepily. When it rose, he stopped whatever he was doing, as if to listen to words Nya could not hear. She had asked him once what—or who—he listened for, and he had replied with one word: power. The answer had surprised her, but maybe it shouldn't have.

What would he hear in the Witterkin?

Her eyes opened, and she stared pensively out the window. "Yasna, have you ever heard of the Witterkin changing?"

"Never." Her hands stilled. "Why do you ask? Did you see something?"

"No." It was true. She hadn't *seen* anything.

Yasna's nails clicked again. "Everything changes, and what doesn't is holy." After a pause, she chuckled, a rolling sound that came from deep in her chest. "That's what my ma used to say. Maybe it's true, and maybe it's not. Change is a tricky thing. Some things change on their own, and others need something to change them. I'd wager that something could change the Witterkin."

***

Something.

Nya leaned forward in the buggy seat, trying not to touch the twenty braids that now clung to her head in little rows. Yasna had shown her how to weave the ends into a fancy bun and secure it with a ribbon. Nya fingered her scalp, wondering how she would sleep that night with them bulging from the back of her head. And what Goran would think when he saw her.

In the end, she need not have worried about either. Her brother never came home that night, and she slept as soon as her head hit the pillow. She rose early and spent the morning completing the daily tasks that Goran had instructed her to do. Confer with the servants, review the accounts, fulfill orders… None of it should have been difficult, yet by noon, her hands shook, and her eyes pricked with stupid tears. The servants were stiff and unfriendly around her, and she missed her father with a physical ache that welled up without warning.

The moment she was free, she almost ran to her shed. She didn't make it to the workbench before the maid called to say that the Windsinger's helper was at the door.

Of course, he would have to be the same one she had tormented two days earlier.

"How can I help?" she asked gently after his eyes had bulged, probably at the sight of her braids.

He jammed his hands into his armpits and looked around, as if in search of shelter. His words came out in a rush. "Windsinger Yaro wants to take you and Goran up the hill to see the plot. It's a good day for it and all."

"My brother's not here, but I'll see if I can track him down. Would you like to wait in the sitting room?"

"No need, lady. I was only to deliver this message. Come by if you like, anytime today."

She thanked him, and he fled to his horse.

A breeze tugged at Nya's skirt. She pulled her boots on and followed it out the door.

She thought she knew where Goran would be. There was only one vacant farm near the mountain. For some reason, her father had left it to lie fallow. It was a pretty spot, with a nearby well that never went dry. Nya had once sheltered in the ruins of the farm cottage during a thunderstorm, listening to mice and birds shift in the shadowy corners.

And now....

She stopped and stared. The cottage was gone, its stone walls pulled down and replaced by a new foundation at least the size of the Stary manor. Several wagons congregated on the nearby cart road, and workers hauled goods up a cleared path to the work site. She spotted Goran among the workers, his straight-backed profile turned toward some oncoming wooden beams. How had all this been accomplished so quickly? And how could he afford it? Their father had relied on income from tenant farms to pay expenses. He had left them a bit of extra coin he had squirreled away, but not enough to cover the cost of building such a large manor.

With an effort, she shoved the questions aside and approached him. Shouting to him would have only drawn the workers' gazes to her, and she didn't think she could stand their uneasy looks. The boy's had been enough.

"Goran." She touched his arm, bringing his eyes to hers.

"Nya." He sucked in a sharp breath. "What in the name of all the gods did you do to your hair?"

She waved the question away. "Never mind that—"

"Was it Yasna?"

"Listen. Yaro's helper was just by to say we're wanted on the hill today."

He looked behind him at the foundation, then shook his head decisively. "I can't. Not today. And not tomorrow either. I'm busy here. You go."

Her jaw slackened. "Me? Alone?"

He snorted. "Listen to you. May as well be talking about the hangman's noose."

"You don't know what it's like for me in town."

"It's as bad as you make it."

She bit back an angry retort. "It's not just that. This is Father we're talking about. How can you just—"

"Because I'm busy. And I'm not needed up there. Yaro chose the spot, and you said he knew what he was about. Tell him I trust his judgment and that I'll be there when the stone goes in the ground." He started to turn away and then wheeled back. "By the way, Faina and I are to be married. We haven't set a date yet, but there'll be an engagement ball next weekend. You should find something to wear while you're in town. And get rid of those braids. They look like bloody caterpillars."

"Congratulations on your engagement," she called, but her voice was lost in Goran's shouts to his workers.

It was a dreary walk back home. She tried to work loose a braid, but it was so small and stiff that it was like picking apart rope. She would have to get Yasna to remove them.

She halted and gazed up at the clouds scudding across the sky. No, she would not ask. Nor would she find a gown in town. One of her mother's would do, and if Goran didn't want braids or old gowns at his ball, then he wouldn't have her either.

She walked straight past the house and on to the stables. It was a good day for a ride, and if she had to venture into town alone, she wouldn't sit like a toad in a box.

Only when she was trotting down the road did she remember that she still wore her plain belted house frock. What would Yaro think of her?

Gods, was she really about to spend an afternoon with Yaro? She'd been so fixated on the unpleasantness of going into town that she had set him completely from her mind.

She pushed the horse to move faster, and then faster still. Her lips curved in a sickly smile as she gazed sightlessly ahead, feeling stripped to the bone. Raw and free. She did not grimace at people's shouted words and jeering laughter. Did not slow to stare down three huddled women who whispered and pointed. Only when the stone walls of Yaro's workshop reared in her path did she pull up and dismount. Furtively, she wiped her sweaty hands on her skirt. Yaro stood in the doorway, watching her with a bemused smile. He had removed his apron and wore an unbelted jerkin over a loose shirt and gray hose.

His mouth straightened, and he nodded to her as she approached the door. "Should we wait for your demon pursuers before going inside?"

"Let's not."

"Not wait?"

"Go inside."

He leaned against the doorframe and seemed to study her boots. "I guess your brother isn't coming."

"No. Just me."

"Are you up for it?" he said, but she knew he really meant: *Are you up for being with me?*

"If I wasn't, I wouldn't be here."

There was a silence. Nya glanced up at the steep finger of Cemetery Hill. A low, breathy sound swept down from it—the voices of the dead. She sensed his eyes on her again and shifted uncomfortably.

"All right," he said finally, his voice as breathy as the wind. "Let's go."

***

Yaro took the lead on his dappled gelding, letting the horse have its head as it trotted up the winding road to the top of the hill. The Windsinger's dark hair stood up from his head like seaweed in a current, and his loose brown jerkin flapped behind him. Gradually, the familiar sounds of the town diminished, as if a wet cloth had been thrown over the jumble of buildings, docks, and fishing boats, leaving only the song of the dead, played by the wind.

The sound was indescribable. Groups of stones all cut in slightly different ways had been positioned so that when the wind blew through their slits, the tones would harmonize. Add a thudding percussion and an occasional wail, and the result was not merely beautiful, but unearthly. The wind itself played the stones like an invisible bard, not with a steady, unvarying hand, but with rushes of energy, a passion that was almost human.

As they rode the last loop to the top, Yaro peered back at Nya with a grin, doubtless wanting her to feel whatever wild joy rushed through him at the sound. Perhaps it was pride too. The secret to creating singing stones had remained in his family, and therefore in Sundyr. No other town had a hill like this one. She smiled back. And in that instant, the tension between them eased.

"Clouds are rolling in," he called back to her. "And there's a bit of mist on the hill."

They slowed at the top and dismounted. Narrow paths cut lines between the stones, some half overgrown with weeds, others hard-packed and bare. The wind was calm for the moment, leaving the thin mist in its wake. She followed Yaro in silence, listening to the crunching of his boots and trying not to think about her mother, whose unique voice had landed her in a separate section of the hill. Nya had been up here several times in the years since her mother's death, attending first her grandfather's and then her great uncle's stone ceremonies, but the wind had never been as strong as it was on the day her mother's voice was added to the windsong.

As if it had heard her thoughts, the wind stirred, and the mist eddied around the stones. A soft thudding arose, sporadic at first, but growing steadier as the wind off the sea increased. It usually came from the sea, bending the grass and shrubby trees in one direction.

Yaro slowed at an empty patch of earth and looked back at her.

She asked, "Here?"

He nodded. "The stone will be placed so the wind doesn't hit its face directly. The shape of the hole, together with the stone's angle, will create a thudding sound."

"Like chuckling," she said, nodding. "That's clever."

He flashed her a self-deprecating smile. "I'd like to take the credit, but the idea was my grandfather's."

"You haven't added some new sounds to the song?" She thought back to the freshly inked areas on the old map of the cemetery on his workshop wall.

He shrugged. "I'm working on something. Don't know how it will sound yet or how people will take to it, but…" He trailed off and chuckled. "It's an odd business, waiting for death so you can make music. I don't know what to think of myself sometimes." His eyes pulled at hers, wanting something from her. Understanding, perhaps. Or acceptance.

When she didn't answer, he shrugged again, walked a few steps, and stooped to pick up a small wooden box. There was a tiny squeak and scratching of claws as he lifted it.

"Is that a rat?" she asked, relieved at the change in topic.

He leaned in. "At least one. Folks don't like rats in the cemetery, so—"

"So you trap them instead of poisoning them."

"There's enough death in my work."

"What do you do with them?"

"I loose them at the harbor, where they'll probably be poisoned anyway, but at least it won't be at my hand." He tucked the box under one arm and then wandered around, lifting other boxes and setting them down if they were empty.

Nya watched him bemusedly. He was so careful not to jostle the box as he stooped. So gentle with a beast that most men would crush under their feet. But he had always been like that. He had not changed at all.

She looked away, swallowing back a dryness in her throat. All the girlish feelings she'd once had for him surged back, as inexorable as the wind. She breathed carefully, waiting for them to subside, but they did not. Perhaps they never truly would. She shouldn't have come up here with him alone.

A raindrop fell on her mouth. She pushed her lips together, tasting it. Wanting more. Rain would be a reason to leave.

In the end, she got her wish. Without saying much, they both mounted and returned to the road that wound down the hill. The sky had changed to a dull iron gray. Cold rain pelted down, sometimes turning sideways in the wind gusts.

Yaro's hair was plastered to his neck and face as he pulled up to the workshop. He glanced back at her. "Come in and dry off a bit."

She wanted to. Gods, but she wanted to. The more she was with him, the more she wanted to be.

She shook her head. "Thanks, but I think the rain is setting in. Not much chance of waiting it out."

He dismounted and approached her. "I never asked how you were."

"I'm fine."

He nodded, running a hand over her horse's flank. He was going to say more, she thought. Drag back the past and cause them both pain. She saw it in the way he held his mouth, in the tightness around his eyes.

"Thank you," she said abruptly, "for taking me to see the plot. Let us know when the stone is finished. Goran will come, if I have to drag him by his scruff." She gave him a swift, awkward smile, and then left him alone in the empty road.

The journey back home was a rain-sodden blur. She rode through the lonely streets, passing cottages shuttered against the wind and rain. By the time she passed the horse to her stableman, she was wet through and shivering.

A hot bath and warm meal did little to shake off the chill.

When it was close to midnight, she rose from bed and made her way to the great fireplace in the hall. Her brother was still up, sipping brandy from a crystal cup in his high-backed chair. His eyes were full of flames as he glanced at her. "You didn't get rid of the braids."

She almost laughed. Instead, she took a chair beside him and leaned into the fire. "Am I a child or an adult, Goran?"

His mouth opened and then closed again. He couldn't say she was a child, not after giving her the Stary estate and all the responsibilities that went with it.

"From now on," she said quietly, "I will dress my hair and body as I please."

Wood snapped, punctuating her words. Goran said nothing.

After a long pause, Nya began to worry that she had damaged what little warmth they had. Only a few people in the world cared about her. Would she sacrifice her brother's friendship in order to hold on to this bit of freedom? She searched for something to say. She could talk about their father's plot, but that would remind Goran of the other argument they had had.

"The Witterkin have changed," she blurted at last. "Have you noticed?"

"What?" He jolted as if wakened from sleep. "No. I mean, I haven't seen them lately. Have you?"

"I saw them yesterday. They sound different. Low, and sort of menacing."

"You should stay away from them." He gulped down the last of his brandy and stood up, swaying a little with drink. "No reason for you to go there now. I'll look in on them."

Leaving her with those words, he strode out of the hall and closed the door.

***

To keep the peace, Nya avoided the Witterkin for the next few days. Doing so was not easy. She was accustomed to visiting them several days a week. She used to make excuses for these frequent visits: that she wanted the exercise, or the fence needed a looking over, or she wished to forage in the area. But eventually, she'd stopped trying to justify it and faced up to the truth—strange as the Witterkin were, she loved spending time with them.

A few days, she thought firmly, *and no more.*

To distract herself, she began experimenting with the yellow-leafed plant. A small amount made for an excellent sleep aid, and more might be used to anesthetise a person during surgery, but for now she had no way to test that possibility. After the ball, she would return to the field and dig up the plant. If she could find it again. She hadn't been in a clear frame of mind when she'd happened on it.

The wind had calmed after the storm, and the air grew so dry and hot that Yasna said it reminded her of her childhood home. The older woman stood at Nya's back once more, this time in Nya's mother's old chamber. Nya's reflection peered relentlessly back at her in a gilded mirror. She wore her mother's cream gown and starched ruffle collar. A thick yellow sash under her breasts concealed the fact that she was less endowed than her mother had been. In all other ways, the gown fit.

Yasna tidied Nya's tiny braids and bound them in a fancy bun at the crown of her head. "I thought you'd tear these out the first chance you got," she said.

"They've grown on me," Nya murmured, falling once more under Yasna's spell of clicking nails and tugging hands. She wished she could stay in the chair all evening. Goran wasn't holding the ball in their spacious dining hall, as she'd hoped. Instead, he had rented Bell Hall and invited half the town. And Nya was supposed to brave it all as if she were a flake of sunlight come down like a blessing.

Yasna stared at the mirror and dropped her hands. "My, but you look well, Nitty. Just smile a little, and no one will treat you badly."

***

Smile.

Nya tried as she slipped through the hall's massive doors and sought out the nearest shadowy corner. Her lips strained over her jutting dogteeth, holding them captive while she looked from the doorman to the groups of people chatting together. Goran glanced at her from across the hall, nodded, and looked away.

Bell Hall was like a giant, fancy barn. Some said it was the oldest building in town, and it was easy to believe, with its arching roof supported by bare wooden beams and its steep stained glass windows.

Nya found the old bench she had sat on years ago and traced the delicate carvings along its arms. Memories flooded back. If she looked up, she was sure she would see her mother again, slender and smiling, waving her over. And Yaro. She could almost feel the warmth of his large body at her side, smell a hint of windstone dust and whatever spice he used to wear. She forced herself to sit still and breathe. To focus on the here and now.

Fortunately, no one bothered her.

The townsfolk were not as well decked out as they had been when she was a girl. A gold mine in the mountains had caved in nine years earlier, ending what had been a decades-old source of income for several families. Attempts to excavate the ruins had failed, and while there was still talk of restoring the mine, no one truly believed it could be done.

A small smile touched her lips. One thing had not changed: the size of the codpieces. If anything, they had grown, jutting under pot bellies and between the folds of embroidered jerkins, or bulging between chicken legs like an egg ready to hatch.

The evening passed more pleasantly than she had anticipated. Servers offered her wine and cuts of meat. Minstrels in the gallery played rousing tunes with drums and pipes, and her brother made himself the center of it all. He and Faina danced with abandon, their red and white garments matching to perfection.

She saw Yaro, then. He wore a deep blue-green jerkin, the color so rich and the cut so fine and well fitted that it seemed shaped by magic. He stood to one side, talking intently with two elderly men and a boy. Had he come late? Must have. She had been watching for him all night, worrying what she would do if he planted himself beside her on the bench, wanting to dredge up the past. After a few moments, she threw back the last of her wine and slipped outside.

Bell Hall sat on a cliff overlooking the sea. Its torchlit back patio was of polished flagstone. A dry stone wall encircled it, keeping party-goers from venturing too close to the cliff edge.

Nya leaned on the wall, holding herself against the chill. A silvery moon rose over the waves, casting a smudge of light on the water. Strands that had come loose from a braid brushed her cheek. She let them linger at her lips before swiping them away.

"Nya."

Yaro's deep voice seemed to emerge from the water. Reluctantly, she turned to where he stood beside her…and then took a half step back. Something in his eyes and the stiff set of his shoulders made her heart jolt in her chest.

He didn't seem to notice her alarm, or perhaps he chose not to. He said, "I heard that Goran gave you the manor and took the land at the mountain for himself."

It wasn't phrased as a question, but she nodded anyway.

He sighed and leaned away from the wall. "There's a rumor. The boy who works for me overheard something.

The…information was serious enough that I approached the source to ask about it. The man denied it, but there was fear in his eyes when he spoke, and the next day my lad had bruises on his face. So…" He rubbed the back of his neck.

"What?" She leaned in, all awkwardness gone. The boy's face had been uninjured when he'd stopped by a few days ago, so this must have just happened. "What is the rumor?"

He glanced back at the patio, as if to ensure they were alone. "It's that your brother has found a new mine in the mountain."

She laughed out a tight breath she'd been holding. "Is that all?"

Yaro didn't reply. He merely looked at her, his expression dark and serious.

"It's impossible," she said. "I know the land he has now, and there's no way into the mountain. I mean, there might be an entrance on the other side of the Witterkin, but…"

"So there's no gap in them?"

"No." The only gap she knew of was at the old caved-in mine, a good twenty miles from the Stary property.

"And he couldn't have…tunneled underneath them?"

"Again, no. They lie at the foot of the mountain, Yaro. On solid stone."

His eyes closed, and he pinched the space between his brows. "That's what I thought."

"Then what are you suggesting? That he…he…" She shook her head, went still, and then shook it again. A menacing note drifted into her mind—the Witterkin's eerie warning. "No. He couldn't have. I mean, he wouldn't have hurt the Witterkin."

After a long and terrible silence, Yaro whispered, "I spoke to some others tonight. No one admits to hearing the rumor, but their eyes say something else. Something dark is going on. I'd report it, but I don't have any real evidence."

Evidence. She gave a weary nod. "I'll walk the fence at Goran's property tomorrow."

"Be careful."

"The Witterkin don't hurt you if—"

"Not of the Witterkin. Of people. Gold can make men mad."

She licked her suddenly dry lips. "Thank you. For trusting me."

His shoulders loosened from their stiff line. "Always."

CHAPTER THREE

Nya struggled to sleep that night. As time passed, the terrible possibility that Yaro had hinted at took form, like some monstrous beast rising out of shadow and moonlight. Every objection she raised shredded as soon as it formed. Goran would not have feared the watchman who walked the Witterkin fence, because they were friends. The watchman might even be in on the mine. Nor would selling the gold present a difficulty—a merchant trade in gold had already been established years before. It would take nothing more than the promise of wealth to start it up again. As for the expense of opening the mine, if enough people were involved, the funds could've easily been found.

Imagining *how* he might've cleared a path through the Witterkin was even worse than asking *if*... The court's fine for disturbing them was meant to deter daredevils and vandals. Nya had no idea what sort of punishment awaited those who destroyed a whole swath of them.

"Goran," she whispered to the darkness. Had she known her half brother at all?

She pushed her face into the pillow and managed at length to drift off.

The following morning was far busier than she had anticipated. By noon, not fewer than eleven women had dropped by to purchase hillwort for hangovers. *Amazing,* she thought, *how civil people can be when they want something.* One had even managed a tight smile.

It was near the supper hour before Nya found the courage to walk toward the mountain. An empty vodka bottle left on the fireplace mantle had indicated that Goran had returned sometime in the night, only to take off again while she slept—strange behavior for someone who had stayed up late drinking and dancing. Nya had hoped he would sleep late into the day, allowing her to walk the Witterkin fence in peace. Now she'd likely have no choice but to confront him. Perhaps she should ask what he thought about the idea of looking for an entrance into the mountain. His answer might tell her whether or not this scheme even existed. After that... She kicked at a rock in the road. She would have to investigate the Witterkin at night, when no one was around.

Goran's property looked abandoned from a distance. The road was bare, the path leading up to it empty of horse-drawn wagons and building material. The foundation looked the same as it had before. All the lumber had evidently gone to the creation of a single outbuilding, several yards from the manor's foundation. A gray cloud passed over the sun, casting darkness on the scene. Nya folded her arms and shivered despite the late afternoon's warmth. She strode past the foundation to the outbuilding and tugged on a padlock that held its double doors closed. No sounds emanated from within, not even the shuffling of a horse.

"Goran!" She circled around it, strands of hair blowing into her eyes. When she came to the doors again, her gaze fell on a wagon track leading away from the outbuilding toward the mountain. Nya took a small step, and then another, her boots sinking into the muddy tracks left by wagon wheels.

She followed the track until it neared the Witterkin fence. From there, it veered right and disappeared down a slope. Nya knew that nothing of interest lay beyond that slope. More Witterkin. The mountain. She drew a chill hand over her forehead. If Goran and his friends weren't at the outbuildings, then they were at the end of this track. She didn't know what they would do to her if she witnessed their crime. She'd like to think that Goran would protect her from his friends, but could he really control everyone involved in this scheme? *Gold can make men mad.*

Had madness taken her brother? She made a small sound in her throat. The breathy wail of the Witterkin filled her with foreboding.

Her legs felt rubbery as she raced home.

The moment she stepped inside, the maid informed her that Yasna was waiting for her.

"I brought some fresh strawberries," the older lady announced as Nya entered the sitting room. Yasna sat with crossed legs on a divan, her riding cape still draped over her shoulders.

"That's...thank you."

Yasna's smile fell. "What happened?"

Nya told her everything. Afterward, Yasna crossed to the room's fireplace and ran a fingernail over the blackened stone. "This is quite serious, Nitty."

"I know. There was a feeling of...of evil about that place." Or maybe it was just her own fear.

Yasna's fingernail dragged to a stop. "My mother's folk used to tell tales of evil taking on flesh and becoming a beast."

Nya hissed out a nervous laugh. "I think it visited me last night."

"This is no joke."

"I didn't think it—"

"That's right. You didn't think. And neither did Yaromir, sending you out there alone."

"He didn't send me, I—"

"Doesn't matter. He should have offered to come." She paced back to the chair, stared at the berry basket for a few moments, and then looked hard at Nya. "I'll stay here with you until Goran comes home, then we'll sneak out and follow the track together. If what's there is what we think is there, we'll go to the sheriff."

"No." She looked aside from the stern brown eyes. "Let me talk to Goran first."

"That wouldn't be wise, Nitty."

"Why? He's still my brother. He wouldn't..." Nya swallowed sharply and folded her hands tightly in her lap.

Yasna laid a comforting hand on her shoulder. "You're right, he wouldn't hurt you, but he might try to bring you into his plan, and if you refuse, he might set a watch on you and keep you from going into town."

Nya stared at the blackened mantle, envisioning it. At length, she said, "I'll fetch Yaro tomorrow, and we'll follow the track together." She had expected Yasna to demand that she come too; instead, the older lady slipped her fingers into the folds of her riding cape and drew out a sheathed knife.

"I can spare this for a few days. Take it," she urged, pushing the polished wooden handle into Nya's hand. "You need to defend yourself if the need arises."

Nya gaped at it, taken aback by the thought that Yasna kept a hidden knife in some secret pocket of her cape. Then she opened it and saw that it was double-bladed.

"It's a dagger," Yasna said. "And sharp, mind you, so be careful."

Nya ran a finger down the flat of the blade. She shivered inside at the thought of drawing blood with it. "Do you believe that tale about evil becoming a beast?"

"Of course not. There's no need for beasts when we've got people mucking about. Now..." She took the blade from Nya and held it poised in the air. Her long, tapered fingernails looked themselves like tiny daggers. "I'll show you how to use it."

She left an hour after nightfall, her cape billowing in the evening breeze.

Nya stared after her receding buggy, half wishing that her friend had stayed. The manor seemed to creak with emptiness. Nya grazed the carvings on the banister as she climbed the stairs to her room, feeling stems, buds, leaves under her fingers.

She woke to silence at the darkest hour. She had not heard Goran come home. Was he sleeping in his outbuilding now? She drifted through the house, opening doors. The dining hall was dark and empty; not a coal flickered in the hearth.

Goran's chamber door came open at a touch. She stood in its silence, a drift of the exotic perfumes he wore tickling her nostrils. The curtains hung open. She paused before closing them, her gaze lingering on the gauzy fingernail of the moon. "Something's happened to him," she whispered before darker clouds blew over and the light in the sky went out.

***

She was up and dressed before dawn. The cook huffed at having to prepare breakfast so early, but an extra spending coin smoothed her tight lips. Nya was halfway to the stables when the sound of an approaching rider made her turn.

Yaro, dressed in a loose leather jerkin and tall boots, dismounted and walked his horse toward her. "Have you walked the fence yet?"

"No."

"Good." His shoulders relaxed, and he leaned a hand on the butt of some sort of blade hooked to his belt. Nya had never seen him wear a weapon, and she was taken aback by how dangerous his large, callused hand looked resting on it. "I shouldn't have asked you to go alone," he said. "I don't know what I was thinking."

The words echoed Yasna's so cleanly that Nya grinned. "Forget it. Let's just go."

He glanced around. "Now? Goran—"

"Is missing. He's spent the night away before, but this feels different. I'm worried that something might have happened to him...wherever he is."

As they rode up the road that led to the path to Goran's property, Nya recounted what she had seen there. Then she spoke about the dagger and Yasna's fear of what Goran might do if Nya confronted him about the mine. Yaro, riding close behind her, never interrupted her harried string of words. Maybe he was remembering the first time she had sat beside him at Bell Hall. She had been so nervous of him then that she hadn't stopped chattering. And he had just sat there, nodding along as if she weren't a freak.

The property was still deserted. Nya's hands were ice-cold as she dismounted and walked her horse around the outbuilding. She paused at the track and crouched down to examine the drying mud. "No one's been here since yesterday afternoon," she muttered to Yaro's leaning shadow.

"Then let's follow the path," he suggested quietly and nudged his horse into the lead.

It was a short ride to the Witterkin fence. Nya had expected Yaro to turn and continue along the track, so she was startled when he pulled up. His eyes were wide when he looked back at her. "The Witterkin sound different."

Nya winced. She had completely forgotten the fact that he didn't know. "Yes."

He continued to look at her. "How long have you known?"

"Since the day my father died. I don't know how far the change extends."

"Probably not far, if it's been two weeks."

Two weeks. She should have told him at Goran's ball. Why hadn't she? She opened her mouth to explain, but he was already turning his horse and heading toward the spot where the land dipped down.

She followed him at a trot and almost passed him when he halted once more. They had reached the top of the slope. At the bottom, the ring of Witterkin thinned to a narrow strip of forty feet wide. The mountain loomed over them, dark against the blue sky. Nya had visited this tucked-away corner of her family's property numerous times before. She knew every plank of wood in the fence and the various plants that grew in the field alongside it.

And it had all changed.

A large swath of the Witterkin was no longer green, but a deep scarlet red. It was the color of pain, and the sound emanating from it had a desperate, serrated edge. The reason for the Witterkin's mourning was all too clear: A shadowy path had been cut through them, creating a walkway between the field and the base of the mountain.

As shocking as all this was, it paled next to the most frightening change of all—the red Witterkin had broken through the fence to the field beyond. Nya judged they had expanded at least twenty feet. Why they hadn't filled in the path was a mystery to her. Perhaps they had left it out of respect for the dead, or perhaps the path had been wider than it was now.

"I can see them moving," Yaro whispered, his voice hollow.

Her head jerked toward him. "Moving?"

"Or spreading. Call it what you like. But they aren't finished yet, and I don't know now if they ever will be."

As Nya refocused in horror on the seeping red, a sudden stab of fear for her brother jolted through her. She cupped her hands around her mouth and shouted his name, again and again. When there was no answer, she took off down the slope, ignoring Yaro's shouted warning.

Her horse blew and tensed as they neared the scarlet Witterkin. Nya steered him well around it, dismounted, and then started down the path. She paused where the Witterkin had perished, her nose wrinkling at a foul, poisonous scent wafting up from the oily rock under her feet. Had Goran poisoned these ones? If so, where had he disposed of them?

"Don't!" Yaro pleaded behind her. "Come back, and I'll go."

She shook her head jerkily. "I can't."

Her heart thundered as she jogged up the path toward a gap in the rock wall. Several empty barrels lay on their sides behind a boulder, one still oozing a dark, oily liquid. Her suspicion that the Witterkin had been poisoned grew to near certainty. Yaro's footsteps thudded close behind her. Together, they scrambled up muddy boulders, through the tall, narrow gap and on into a sizable cave.

Light from the gap streamed inside, casting a brilliant band on the floor, which was not bare, but covered with scarlet Witterkin. Their menacing sound echoed off the rock walls so that it was one continuous thrum. A narrow path ran through them, stinking with the poison smell. The path ended at a glittering rock wall. And it was there that Goran and two others had met their end.

The three bodies, half covered in Witterkin, lay at odd angles on the floor. Nya screamed at her brother's empty eyes and mottled skin, screamed until her throat was raw and she didn't know where her voice ended and the

Witterkin's began; it was all one ragged sound. Yaro gripped her forearms and held her to him with a bruising strength.

After a cold, endless moment, he warned, "We can't stay here."

Nya had ceased screaming and was almost still, her face pressed into her hands. Her stomach roiled, threatening to yield up the breakfast she had so dutifully eaten. Flies buzzed, and her nose wrinkled at a hint of rot in the air. Yaro's arms fell, and the warmth at her back vanished. "Let's go," he said.

"What if he's not truly dead?" she choked.

"He is. They are. I've seen enough corpses to know that." He touched her shoulder. "I'm sorry, Nya."

He stayed close to her as they trudged out of the cave and then down the blackened path. "Did you recognize the other two corpses?" he asked, slowing to look back at her.

"Yes. They were two of my brother's friends, Enis and Frane."

He nodded and walked on with a lowered head.

Nya's eyes filled with tears. She should have continued on to the mine yesterday. If she had, Goran might still be alive. Why hadn't she? Because of her stupid fear?

"Don't," Yaro said harshly as they walked the horses up the slope.

"Don't what?"

"*Don't* play the what-if game. It'll eat at your soul until you're no better off than those corpses."

An old pain flickered in his eyes. Nya swallowed tightly and looked away from it.

They didn't speak again until they were back at the Stary manor. Nya dismounted first and stared at the looming shadow of her family's home. She lowered her head into the horse's flank, willing it all away.

Yaro's hand closed on her back. "You shouldn't be alone now. Let me fetch Yasna."

She shook her head, not trusting herself to speak.

Yaro said, "Is there someone else who—"

"No."

After a silence, he took his hand away. His boots crunched on the rocky pavement as he paced nearby. "I don't want to leave you alone, but there's something I have to do. If it works, it might stop the Witterkin from spreading."

A door closed somewhere, and the stableman lumbered over, his game leg giving him away. Nya, blinking her eyes dry, let him lead her mare to the water trough. He returned soon after for Yaro's spotted gelding.

When they were alone again, Yaro whispered, "I'll be back tomorrow morning. If you're feeling up to it then, we can ride back to the mine."

They were standing very close. In half a breath, Nya could step into his arms, and he would not question it. Had she reached the limit of her strength?

She cleared her throat and sought to order her thoughts. "You want to go back there. Why? What are you planning?"

"It's just an idea. Can you wait until tomorrow before reporting what we saw?"

She sighed. "I hadn't even thought of reporting it. My mind is a muddle." She pushed a hand hard against her eyes. "Yes, I can. Willingly."

"Good. Tomorrow, then." He started to turn and then paused and looked back at her. "It would be best if you told the maid to turn away visitors. Have her say you're in town, or some other place. Just don't have her let on that you're at home."

Her eyes widened. "Do you think I'm in danger?"

"I don't know. I'm going to sniff around a bit this afternoon before I start on my...project, see if I can find out if others were involved in the mine."

Nya rubbed the space between her brows. "All right. I'll do as you say."

She thought he might linger with her for a while longer. Half of her wished he would. Instead, he fetched his horse from the trough and trotted off down the road without a backward glance.

The rest of the day was a blur. The maid accepted her order with a raised brow and pursed lips. Later, she told Nya, who had holed herself up in her work shed, that half a dozen people had stopped by, most claiming to want herbs. The wives of Enis and Frane had been among the visitors. Nya wanted to ask how the women had looked but didn't think she could bear the answer. They had requested valerian root, which was used for stress and sleeplessness. She hoped they went to the apothecary. His prices were steeper, but he was usually well stocked.

Darkness fell. She had expected to be up all night mourning her brother, but the scarlet Witterkin snatched Goran from her mind. In her dreams, they spread faster and faster, a red river gushing over the fields toward her home, and then it was inside, slipping through cracks and under doors, filling the quiet rooms with accusing voices. She woke, icy cold and trembling, her face wet with tears.

She did not weep for Goran.

All her life, she had admired the Witterkin. They had been her escape, her touch of magic in a mundane world. Now all that had been taken from her, to be replaced by the horror of seeing her brother dead. She would never again be able to stare into their depths without reserve, and if Yaro's idea failed...

Her hands clenched under the covers. This was all Goran's fault. He had lied to her about why he wanted that land. The new house had been a prop. Maybe he had not even intended to finish it. After all, once he had mined enough gold, he could buy the Stary manor from her for a fair price, along with whatever else he wanted.

"Why didn't I see through it?" she whispered to the ceiling.

***

Yaro arrived on a wagon shortly before noon the next day. His eyes were deeply shadowed, and he smelled of stone dust and sweat. Nya was not much better. Goran's fiancée had dropped by early that morning and wouldn't leave the doorstep until Nya appeared. Her normally tidy blonde hair had been askew and her clothing rumpled. Even her expensive pink satchel was smudged with dirt. She had just returned from Goran's property, she said, when Nya grudgingly came to the door, and he was not there. So where was he? He wouldn't have just disappeared while they were in the midst of arranging a wedding. But he hadn't made his appointment with the seamstress yesterday, so where was he?

Nya merely shrugged and said that he had not been home. "But look through the place if you like," she offered. Faina did so, and more thoroughly than Nya had expected. By the end, she was panting and close to tears.

Nya watched her ride off with wide, frozen eyes. How could she tell Faina what had really happened?

Maybe she wouldn't have to. In a short time, the whole town would know what Goran had done and what had become of him, and the Stary name would be forever tarnished. Faina would recover and maybe even congratulate herself on her escape.

Yaro greeted her in the doorway with a tired smile, his large body haloed in light. His eyes widened when they fell on her strained face, but he was wise enough not to ask how she was. "Well…" He looked down at the floor between them. "I did it. Took me all night and then some, but it'll do what I want it to do. Whether or not the Witterkin respond is another question."

"What did you make?"

"A bit of magic." He grinned again and nodded toward the wagon. "That's what I'll call it if it works. Let's go."

Nya, grateful to leave the house, put on her belt pouch and boots, and hurried out the door. She was curious about the "sniffing around" he'd said he would do, but it didn't seem the right time to ask about it.

They mounted Yaro's wagon seat, and he guided the horses back toward the road. The turnoff came quickly, and the wheels jolted as they encountered potholes and rocks. The wagon creaked and rattled in response, making conversation impossible. Still, Nya glanced at Yaro often. She had never seen him so abuzz with energy. It was as if he burned from the inside—a warm, sparkling light that blazed on her whenever he met her eyes. It was passion and power. Nya knew the feeling well—it was akin to the heady rush of excitement that came over her when she found a new plant and sensed it would be significant.

He slowed the horses when they reached the abandoned outbuilding, his head bent as he examined the ground.

"Faina visited me this morning," Nya informed him. "She said she was here, but I doubt she followed the track.

If she had, she would've said something about the red Witterkin."

"That's one possibility." His brows pulled together in a thoughtful frown. "I'm no tracker, but it looks like another wagon came through here and went on up the track. Do you see how the clean ruts from my wheels are broken?"

Nya stared at the tracks but could make neither heads nor tails of them. She wasn't even sure which belonged to Yaro's wagon. When she didn't answer, he made a clicking sound, and the wagon rattled again to life.

The top of the slope approached. Nya gripped the wagon seat with white-knuckled fingers. She tried not to dwell on images from her dreams, but they clawed back anyway. In the end, the only thing that banished them was seeing the scarlet Witterkin once more.

Yaro pulled up and stared down the slope, his lips slightly parted. He cleared his throat. "They've moved again. Maybe a couple of yards."

Nya made a sound of agreement. The uneven scarlet lines bled over the track and into the green field. Another section of fence had toppled over, and a faint creaking sound warned of more destruction to come.

Yaro got out and opened the wagon's tail board. "I'm going to leave the wagon up here. No reason to spook the horses. Can you help me carry something down the slope? It's bulky but not heavy."

Things to do. Her stiff fingers loosened, and she stepped off. Yaro closed the tail board and hauled a heavy pack onto his back. Nya lifted the larger pack off the ground where Yaro had deposited it, wincing as its contents creaked.

"Don't worry, you can't hurt it," he assured her.

"What is it?"

Wind stirred his dark, bushy hair. "It's a bellows, of sorts."

A bellows… Nya looked more closely at the sagging weight at his back. Her skin prickled. "You've made a windstone for the dead Witterkin." Even whispered, the words felt too loud, as if she had shouted them.

He gave a slow nod. "The living need to mourn and to remember their voices."

The crackle of enthusiasm was there again, glittering in his eyes.

Could Yaro recreate the Witterkin's lost voices from a stone and bellows?

Yes, she thought. He could.

A shiver of anticipation ran through her at the thought of watching him try, but as they reached the path at the bottom of the slope, Yaro dashed that hope.

He held out his arm. "I'll take the pack now."

Nya shrugged it off and passed it to him. "Are you setting this up here?"

He shook his head. "I have to do this in the cave, where the resonance will be right. If the Witterkin can communicate with each other, then something good might happen. If not…" He sighed and glanced back at the cave. "Either way, this is dangerous. I don't know how they'll react. The path might close, or I might get trampled. If I don't come back after fifteen minutes, I want you to get help."

"No." She snatched the pack back from him. "I'm going with you."

His empty hands fell to his sides. "Then I won't do it. I won't risk your life as well as mine."

Her jaw clenched, and she folded her arms over the pack. "Why risk your life at all? And for something my brother did?"

"Because that's just the way it is."

She stepped closer. "This is my land now."

"Yes, but the Witterkin don't belong to you, no more than I do for standing on your property. Let me help them, Nya." He laid his hand on the pack between them, and their eyes locked in a silent battle.

Of course, he won. Or he thought he won. With a dramatic sigh, she thrust the pack into his arms. Yaro looked as if he would say something more; instead, he started up the path toward the cave. Before he disappeared into the gap, he glanced back at her. He knew her that well. Satisfied that she had not moved, he vanished through the gap.

Nya counted to ten and then sprinted up the path, her legs weak from dread. The thought of glimpsing Goran's corpse again was the least of it. In her mind, the path closed behind her and the Witterkin's menacing sigh grew. She paused at the boulders to catch her breath and then crept up toward the gap as silently as a spider. Yaro was right. She couldn't stop him from doing as he wished. But *he* couldn't stop *her* either.

She padded through the narrow entrance to the cave and edged around a wall. Dust motes floated in the thick beam of light shining from the crack above her; where it landed was now entirely red. The Witterkin had spread in the cave as well. She could still make out bits of the three corpses, but the Witterkin had nearly engulfed them. She swallowed and covered her nose. The smell of rot had intensified since yesterday.

A click of metal against stone echoed off the steep walls. Nya poked her head farther into the cave. At last, she spied Yaro. He was crouched over the windstone and bellows, as close to the cave wall as he could get. The Witterkin were a scant yard from him, but he did not seem bothered by that. Another click, and he straightened a bit. His arms drew back, and he grew as still as stone. When he finally moved again, a high-pitched sighing joined itself to the Witterkin's menacing echo. It seemed to have no source, and if it were not for the tell-tale movement of Yaro's arms, she wouldn't have believed it came from him. Nya had witnessed a demonstration of his windsinging before. The movement of the bellows always caused a fluctuation of sound. In this space, none existed.

Nya clenched her trembling hands together and listened. For several seconds, nothing happened. The Witterkin's wail and Yaro's playing bumped awkwardly together in a dissonant chord. Then they began to merge. Little by little, the Witterkin's voice rose in pitch to meet the windsong's tone. Nya could feel the brush of air blown through the stone now. In the beam of light, it became a living thing, stirring the motes into a mesmerizing storm.

Just as the two sounds met, Yaro swayed like he was about to pass out. Terrified he would fall, Nya raced along the wall toward him. She had only taken three steps when dizziness struck her. She reeled against the wall, her head in her hands. Her ears felt strange, as if they were blocked, and the Witterkin sang inside her instead of outside. But that didn't make sense. With an effort, she shuffled along the wall toward Yaro. He was gripping his head too, one hand brushing the floor as if in search of a handhold. She had just reached him when he fell forward, his head disappearing into the Witterkin.

Nya gripped his waist and pulled, but it was like trying to move the mountain itself. She had no strength. She felt for the hilt of Yasna's dagger and drew it. Anything. She would do anything to save him. Her arm shook wildly as she stabbed at the Witterkin's flickering depths. They were green now. When had they changed from red?

Something brushed her. Light. Wind. A memory. Then all feeling vanished, and she sank into oblivion.

PART TWO:

THE FABRIC

CHAPTER FOUR

Nya woke with sunlight on her face and wiry weeds tangled in her hair. She must have passed out while trying to help Yaro. And then Yaro woke and dragged her out of the cave? His windsinging carried on, its volume rising and falling slightly as he worked the bellows. Relieved to find the dizziness gone, she brushed the weeds off her and sat up.

For a few moments, she did not know what she was seeing. A hilly meadow opened before her, edged by a spectral ridge of mountains. Patches of Witterkin lay here and there like green stains on the meadow's purple carpet. Nya breathed through fingers she had pressed to her mouth. Where in the world was she? "Yaro?"

A female chuckle sounded from behind her. "Why, it's herself, awake and lively." Footsteps thudded and the weeds rustled. Nya felt for her dagger, but it was gone. She must have left it in the Witterkin. Another chuckle, and the silken voice went on, "You look frightened, dearie. You shouldn't be. If I wanted to hurt you, I would have done it while you were still sleeping."

When at last the owner of the voice came into view, Nya let out a squeak of shock. A golden beast stood upright before her. She had a lion's hind legs and a woman's upper body, but the two melded so well that the combination seemed natural. Her hair was twisted back from her face and bound with colored beads and other shiny objects. More beads ringed her neck and wrists. Next to the silken gold of her skin, the decorations looked tawdry. Her tail, which peeked from a hole in her short frock, twitched like a cat's.

Nya was so struck by her appearance that she did not notice the dagger—Yasna's dagger—until the creature lifted it to the sunlight.

"This is a pretty thing," she said, running her finger over a jewel embedded in its hilt. "And I do love pretty things."

It took Nya three tries before she could speak. "That's mine. I mean, it isn't mine, but it's not yours either."

The creature shrugged. "You can try to take it if you like, but I don't suggest it." She twirled the unsheathed knife in her golden fingers. The graceful blade play made Nya's previous efforts with the dagger seem clumsy. "For one thing, you're smaller and weaker than me, and for another, it wouldn't be nice. I risked my life dragging you out of the Witterkin, and if you can't let me have such a small thing in return, then you're not a nice person, and I don't wish to know you."

Nya rubbed at her eyes. Nothing made sense. She had just been with Yaro in the cave, trying to cut Witterkin away from his head. And now she was in a patch of purple weeds in some other place, and Yaro…

She got to her feet and looked behind her. A large patch of Witterkin lay in their purple blanket only a dozen yards off. "Are those the ones you dragged me from?"

"Yes. Don't go back to them!" the creature warned as Nya walked over. "Those were red a short while ago, and they didn't sound cheery."

Nya halted a few feet away, listening to their even, high-pitched sighing. No tell-tale lump of a body marred their perfection. No corpses. No Yaro.

Of course no Yaro. As close as she was to the Witterkin, she could still make out the distinct rise and fall of his windsinging. Without the cave's echo, it was unmistakeably his.

Yaro wasn't lying dead or unconscious in the Witterkin; he was somewhere nearby, playing his heart out. She whirled around, searching the field for him. "Yaro!"

A warm breeze tickled loose hairs against her chin. Where was he? "Where am I?" she begged the creature, who was still absorbed in her knife play.

"Folk call it the Witterwilds," she said absently.

Nya swallowed. "I'm from Sundyr. Ever heard of it?"

"No. But I assume it's in the human world. You *are* human, aren't you?" She glanced up from the dagger and regarded Nya thoughtfully.

"Of course," Nya whispered, rubbing her arms. "What do you mean by 'the human world?' Are you suggesting this place is...is not the human world, but another...?"

"Another world. Yes, you could call it that, dearie."

"I see. And how does one travel between these worlds?"

"I have no idea."

Nya's thoughts scattered as the creature approached her, large paws sliding through weeds to land quietly on the ground. "I've heard," the beast said, "that your world is quite different from ours. The Fabric isn't as loose, so not as many things are possible."

"The Fabric?"

"You've never heard of the Fabric?"

Nya shook her head. "Like you say, I'm not from here." She swallowed again tightly. The beginnings of a headache stirred behind her eyes, and she was on the verge of tears. She had never felt so stranded, so desperate to be home. But even if she found a way back, she couldn't leave without Yaro. *Be strong,* she urged herself. Her life and Yaro's might depend on it. She tried for a friendly smile. "My name is Nya, and..." Her voice broke as the creature jerked back. "What is it?"

"Don't worry, I didn't hear it."

"Didn't hear what?"

"Your name." She poked a clawed finger into Nya's chest. "There's power in a name. *Never* give it freely, least of all to strangers."

"All right." Nya licked her dry lips and started again. "I'm looking for a man named—a man. He's here somewhere, making that high-pitched windsong."

The creature cocked her head, listening. "You're right, it's still there. It's a powerful song, and power gets noticed here."

"Then you were here when it began. Did you see him?"

"No, I never did." She studied the gem on the dagger again, lifting it into the light.

"Do you know where he might be?"

"No."

Nya worried her lip. *It's a powerful song,* the beast had said, *and power gets noticed here.* Was she implying that someone or something had noticed Yaro's playing? "You mentioned power," Nya ventured. "Who notices it?"

A shrug. "I wouldn't know."

Nya turned, swallowing convulsively, her damp gaze finding nothing in the purple field. She resisted shouting Yaro's name again. It hadn't worked the first time, and her throat was so raw that it would probably come out in a gurgle. Who would help her now? She didn't know anything about this place, and the one person who might have helped was a harebrained magpie who had stolen Nya's only weapon. Suddenly she blurted, "You don't need that pretty dagger, or any of the baubles you deck yourself with. They do nothing for you. How can they when you already look like a walking treasure?"

The creature's head lifted, and a bright smile bloomed on her face; she pressed her fingers to her lips as if to hide it. "Do you really mean that?"

"I don't say things I don't mean."

"So kind." She sheathed the dagger and secured it to her painted leather belt. All the while, her tail wagged slowly from side to side. When she was done, she looked past Nya to some point in the distance. "A wind river might lead you to a Windsinger."

"What?"

A strong hand closed on hers. "This way, dearie."

Nya jogged to keep pace with the creature's long, furry legs. Her hand throbbed from being clasped too tightly, and the hem of her frock was being torn to shreds by the sticky weeds, but it didn't matter. Nothing mattered but finding Yaro and getting home. The patch of Witterkin she had been dragged from was swiftly vanishing behind her—a fact that would have disturbed her had Yaro's windsinging faded, but it did not change at all.

After jogging for several minutes, Nya glimpsed a group of golden figures on a distant hilltop. Spotting them, the creature put two fingers to her mouth and whistled out a code. After some moments, her whistle was answered, and she resumed her fast pace.

Nya flung her a nervous glance. Where were they really heading? For all she knew, the beast was escorting her to some sort of killing field, where her friends would join in the feast. Great cats ate flesh. Perhaps Nya had stumbled into her hunting grounds and was now the catch of the day.

As hope drained from her, she began to slow, trampling her dangling hem in the process.

The creature halted. "It was here." Her golden eyes thinned as they swept the purple ground. "I'm sure it was."

"What was here?"

She frowned at Nya. "The wind river. Has it slipped your mind already?" She jerked Nya on without waiting for an answer. A few moments later, she halted again and pointed to some spot just ahead of them. "There it is. Must have shifted last night. No matter. It's there, and it's nice and slow. The wind has been calm lately, but don't let that lull you. It could change again in an hour, so watch the ground as you move. If it starts going faster, then jump off it as soon as you can. If the terrain is not right for jumping, then get down low and wait it out." She paused, evidently waiting for a response.

"I don't understand," Nya admitted. "I don't *see* anything."

The creature took a step and jabbed a clawed finger downward. "Look!"

Nya squinted at the ground. At first, she saw nothing at all, and then her mouth slackened in surprise. A five or six-foot wide band of weeds was continuously shifting, as if moved by invisible hands. She followed the band with her eyes, trying to find its end. But it did not end. It just kept right on going until her vision blurred with her effort to track it. "What is it, a belt made of air? Am I supposed to walk in it?"

"*On* it, dearie, and only if you want to."

"Where does it go?"

"Don't know. I've never followed it to its end." She pulled a painted shell out of her hair and tossed it onto the shifting weeds. When the shell was less than a yard from the ground, it struck something, making a clicking sound. Nya didn't see what happened to it after that. The belt either carried it away or it bounced off into the weeds.

Nya let out a breath she didn't know she had been holding. "So you've ridden it yourself?"

"A few times when it was heading the right way." She tapped her chin. "But I can jump pretty high. It might be harder for you to get on it." She got down on all fours, edged closer to the wind river, and then waved Nya over. "Use my back as a step. It'll be easier that way. Oh, and do something about your dragging skirt."

Nya bent down and tore off her hem with a violent jerk of her wrist.

Was she really going to do this? Only an idiot chased the wind.

Then don't, she thought. *Chase power instead.* If power was important here, then she needed to find whoever took notice of it. The wind river might not bring her to them, but if she rode it long enough, she might find whatever passed here for civilization.

Or it might just lead her to the Windsinger. She couldn't rule out that possibility, as far-fetched as it sounded.

Before she straightened, she plucked the head off a purple weed and tucked it surreptitiously into her belt pouch. Old habits died hard. "Thanks for your help," she said, her feet wobbling as she stepped onto the creature's broad back.

"It's only a foot up, dearie. Try not to touch the edge; it will burn you."

"Is it windy on top, like it is underneath?"

"Not that I recall. Try it and see."

Nya saw nothing but the shifting weeds below. By all rights, she should fall straight down onto them. She closed her eyes and jumped.

At once, she was jerked off balance. She swayed wildly and almost fell. The river's floor felt alive under her feet, as if she stood on a powerful wave about to crash. She took a step and swayed, dizzied by the ground speeding away beneath her. Another slow step. She risked a glance at the meadow, expecting to see the creature running alongside her, but it was empty. Nya was truly alone.

No, that wasn't true. Yaro's windsinging continued, the sound so real and close by that she felt she would see him if she turned her head. Her fists clenched, and she took another step.

Gradually, her balance improved, and she even began looking up to view the landscape. She encountered her first hill before she knew what it was. The land had been sloping up so gradually that she'd barely noticed the incline. And then it hit a peak, or rather a ridge. A sea of jagged rocks and spiny shrubs fell away steeply on the other side. Nya had no time to jump off. Heart in her throat, she braced herself for the descent.

What happened instead was even worse. The river didn't follow the plunging ridge but sailed straight out into the open air. Nya's knees bent, and she almost pitched forward. A scream gathered in her throat, but nothing came out. If only she had jumped earlier. Now, it was too late. The mountains were drawing ever closer, and they were not as even as they had appeared from a distance. Jagged gaps opened like missing teeth in a brawler's mouth, baring nothing but empty blue sky. The wind river was heading toward one of the gaps, its descent excruciatingly slow. Nya was going to sail straight through it and on to whatever drop lay on the opposite side. Her fists clenched on nothingness. She yearned to close her eyes but didn't dare. If she fell now, she would disappear between the giant boulders that lifted their heads toward her. Instead, she spread her arms wide, and as rock walls enclosed her, she finally found her scream.

The sound echoed dizzyingly off the damp walls. She felt a streak of cold shadow, and then the world opened like someone shaking out a blanket, and her scream spluttered in her throat.

At last, she felt the wind. It tore at her hair and clothing, tried to shove her over the edge of nothingness into the blue wash of sky around her. She could do nothing but stand on shaking legs and hope that the river would meet ground again. A sea of jagged rocks lay hundreds of feet below her. Beyond them, green hovered on the horizon. A body of water sparkled in the green until clouds passed over the sun, leaving that distant dream in shadow.

So much for escaping the wilderness. She should have crawled back into the Witterkin where she had been found. Maybe she would have wakened in her own world, next to Yaro. For all she knew, his windsinging was but an echo that had strayed from one world into another, and the longer she remained here, the less likely either of them would survive.

Or not.

And that was hardest of all. Not knowing.

The descent was long and tiring. Nya's throat burned with thirst, and her legs cramped from balancing on the sloping river. She had long ceased walking. Without the belt of swaying weeds beneath her, she couldn't make out the river's edges. A bird wheeled by, mocking her stillness with a fierce cry of pure freedom.

Water. After a time, that was all she could think about. The sun blazed on her bare face, and her eyes, pounded by the wind, felt sticky and swollen. She allowed herself to close them and focused instead on the river's decline.

When it finally leveled off, the scent of sweet, wet grass filled her nostrils. She grinned as her eyes cracked open. Grass swayed alongside her in gentle waves. A band of light, caught between clouds, drifted over the fields and lingered over a blue lake. Nya rode the wind until she neared the shore, then she jumped off into some low grass, managing somehow not to fall. She grimaced as she walked down to the water. Her legs were beyond stiff. If she didn't rest them, she wouldn't be able to walk on the ground, never mind the wind river. She told herself it would be easy to find again—assuming it didn't shift from its location.

The lake was small and clear, bordered by a pebbled beach. A couple of large boulders slouched at its edges, their heads white with bird droppings. As Nya pushed through the grass to the beach, a bizarre sight stopped her in her tracks.

Seven brown robes lay out in a neat row on the shore. She crept closer to them, noting their fine cuts and even seams. They were sized for large men, yet the lake was abandoned. Not so much as a ripple marred its glassy surface. She bent down and nudged a spiderweb that had formed in the hollow of an empty hood. It seemed that the robes had lain there for some time.

Shrugging, she got to her feet, removed her boots and pouch, and waded into the lake. Tiny fish darted away from her legs. Reassured by the presence of life, she bent down and tasted the water. It was refreshingly cold and as sweet as that from any well. She drank deeply from her hands. Afterward, she considered pulling off her sweaty clothing but decided against it. She didn't want to be caught naked if the men returned. Instead, she washed herself clothed in a clumsy fashion, her teeth chattering all the while.

By the time she was finished, she knew she had made a mistake. The sun had vanished under heavy clouds, and she had no means to light a fire. What would she do when night found her, cold, wet, and without food?

Shivering, she walked straight over to the robes, shook one out, and threw it over her shoulders. If no one claimed them before darkness fell, she would strip to her skin and make a bed out of them. She put on her boots and sheltered between the boulders, rubbing her arms until warmth returned to them.

She must have slept a little, for she was wakened by the unwelcome tapping of rain. Moments later, the sound of large, flapping wings filled the air. Pebbles rattled on the beach, and there came a frantic, bird-like screeching. Curious, Nya peered around the boulder toward the clamor.

Her eyes widened. Four tall women with pointed ears and feathered scalps stood on the beach, clothed in the brown robes. Their sharp eyes were fixed on three giant birds of prey. Two of them were wriggling their heads under the remaining robes on the ground. The last bird waddled about in a panic, wings half open. As Nya looked on, the two birds struggling with the robes finally managed to slide them over their heads. And then it was as if they disappeared, their large bodies vanishing under garments much too small to cover them, but moments later, two women poked their heads out of the robes' necks.

The birds had changed into women.

Only one bird remained, its panicked screeching rising to a fevered pitch. Nya knew immediately what she had done. Her stomach churned as she removed the robe and stepped out from her hiding place. "This is yours," she said, not quite keeping out the tremble in her voice. The bird looked to be twenty feet long, and she could only guess at its wingspan.

The sky chose that moment to brighten. All eyes turned toward her. The bird ceased screeching and lowered its head, not in acknowledgement, but as a bull sometimes did before it charged. And that was exactly what it did.

Nya dropped the robe with a squeak and raced for the wind river, but she had only managed a few steps before she was roughly shoved to the ground. Huge wings gusted air over her. She screamed as strong talons closed around her middle, pinching into her belly. The wings beat harder, and the ground fell away. Again.

She struggled to draw breath. "I'm sorry! I didn't know it was yours! Please—"

The bird squeezed tighter, and pain lanced through her. Every breath she drew increased the pain. Where was she being taken? To a nest, where tiny beaks waited for regurgitated meat?

But the bird was not making for the mountains, where such a nest might be. The open grassland raced below her, broken here and there by dark ridges of rock. She had lost sight of the lake and wind river. Abruptly, the bird shifted course and began to fall. Another ridge loomed ahead, or at least that was what Nya took it to be. Was this where she would meet her end?

A fresh wave of strength suffused her. She squirmed in the bird's grip, digging her hands under the deadly talons. The ground was only a few yards away; she might survive the fall if she tumbled in the grass.

The bird screeched and its talons loosened, but just as Nya prepared to fall, the grass vanished and a fissure yawned, like a black mouth open to take her. She wrapped her fingers around a talon and clung on. The bird flapped, and something sharp thumped hard into her back. She lost her grip and plummeted into the dark maw.

CHAPTER FIVE

Nya came very close to landing on the fissure's edge. Instead, she tumbled along one steeply sloped side. Pain lanced through her foot as she hit an outcrop. Bits of stone broke away and fell into the yawning darkness. She tried to snag the outcrop with her other leg, but it slipped away. At last, her hands found a gap in the rock. Her toe found another, and she hung, trembling, as she stared up at the late afternoon sky. A warmth down her leg made her aware that her bladder had let go. "Help!" she screamed. "Please!"

Something rustled nearby. Nya looked to the side but saw nothing. She dug her toe deeper into the gap and blinked away sweat trickling into her eyes.

Small, cool fingers slid down her bare breast. She flinched, her eyes bulging. Horror gathered in her, but she couldn't move away for fear of falling. She looked down at herself in time to watch a doll-sized person wriggle down the front of her frock and latch onto a nipple. It sucked at her for a few moments before spitting the nipple out. The top of the tiny head reappeared.

"Dry as old withered lips," came a high-pitched voice.

"Help!" Nya screamed again. One of her hands was bleeding, making her grip slippy. She scoured the rock above her for a handhold, but there was nothing. Worse, the darkness in the fissure seemed to be deepening. The heavy clouds must have returned. If it rained again, she would be finished.

The creature nestled into the gap between her neck and the rock and spoke. "They say there is a lake of human milk. And only humans know how to reach it. If you promise to take me there, I shall help you."

She scrambled again as her hands slid. "Go away."

"You don't think I can help? Try me. Try me, try me, try—"

"Stop!" Her wounded foot slipped, and she scrabbled for a purchase. She was going to die. Her body would split open on some cold rock in the darkness, and no one would care.

The creature was chittering again, like some sort of demented squirrel. Could he truly help her? Not in her world. But in this one, maybe... "All right."

"Swear on your name. Say you will take me there."

She didn't know where *there* was, but she would promise him anything in exchange for her life. "I swear I'll take you, and that's enough!"

He squealed out a long, high-pitched note that would have made her cringe under different circumstances. "Good. Now, lower yourself down a little and your feet will touch a ledge."

Nya's grip was so precarious that moving even an inch would probably dislodge her. Still, she gritted her teeth and tried. Her free leg stretched as far as it would go... "Nothing!"

"A bit lower."

"I'll fall."

"Then do it. Just let go."

Gasping, she freed her bleeding hand and hung lower. Her toe grazed stone. "There's something!"

"Then let go!"

So she did. And was shocked to find solid stone under her feet.

A sound like tiny claws rasped beside her. "Up! Up!" Following the direction of his voice, she glimpsed the shadowy outline of stone steps leading up from the ledge she stood on. Not a ledge, she corrected wryly, but a step. The stairs continued on down into the darkness, each step only a few inches high but broad enough for human feet. To think they had been right below her the whole time... She pushed the thought aside, unable to process any of it. Least of all that she was still alive and sworn to find a lake of human milk. She climbed the stairs carefully, pain lancing through her injured foot with every step. The creature raced ahead of her.

"Here, stop here. See, there is a gap, and a door." A latch fell, and he disappeared into the rock wall.

Three more steps took her to a deeper space of darkness. She felt the edges of a hole and then bent to crawl into it. A tiny light flared, revealing a rough-hewn cave a couple of feet high and perhaps two yards around. A tiny mattress lay against the far wall; next to it stood a table cluttered with dinner things, all sized for a doll. The creature knelt by a small hearth built into the wall near the cave's opening. A pot and pan hung from a rack above the hearth, and clay jars of various sizes huddled together along the cave walls.

"Please lie down where you can," he said. "I'll make tea."

"I'm afraid that if I do, I'll never get up." Her heart still thrashed in her chest, and she had trouble finding her breath.

"Yes, you will." He spoke with his back to her. "Your promise holds you to it. No, don't close the door. There won't be enough air for you in this space if you do."

Nya nodded and winced as she lowered herself to the floor and spread out. The sticky fabric of her underclothes clung to every injury. If only she had slippery elm bark and some cloth to dress the wounds. The bird creature's talons would not have been clean. She tried flexing her injured foot. It felt swollen, but by some miracle, it wasn't broken.

A pot rattled. "I'll give you my name if you give me yours."

Nya turned her head toward the blazing hearth. Now that she saw her host clearly, she could no longer call him a creature. He was indeed a little person, well proportioned for his foot-high stature, with short blond hair and a smooth, hairless chin. Only his fingernails marked him as different. They were thick and pointed, more like claws than nails. He wore a red tunic over brown hose and pointed, knee-high boots.

She gave him her name.

"Nya," he repeated slowly, as if tasting it. He refocused his attention on the pot. "I am Nenad. How came you to be in this world?"

Nya didn't have the energy to tell the story. "How came you to know I was human?" she countered, her tongue tripping over his odd phrasing. "Have you seen one before?"

"No. But everyone knows what humans look like." After a long pause, he went on. "My people are the Denna. We make spaces deep in the earth, ones larger and more beautiful than this sleeping hole. I am a chima, which means I have no sexual organs. Ah, I see by the look on your face that this shocks you. Or maybe you are shocked by my openness about it. No matter, it is quite common. One in five of my people are born chimas. Many of them wander the wide world. Some have even found new spaces in the ground. Others have discovered extraordinary things."

"Like a lake of milk."

At her mention of the lake, his eyes filmed with desire, and he crooned,

"Ah, the sweet teats of the Lake Mother,

May I drown in her fragrant nectar
And partake of the eternity she bestows
Upon those who drink from her."

Nya's brows rose. "Is that a song of your people?"

He bent once more over the hearth. "Of course not. It's just some foolish twaddle. Your tea is ready." With difficulty, he carried the brimming pot to her and set the handle in her hands. It scarcely held half a cup of tea; still, she thanked him and brought it to her lips. A peppery scent wafted from the steam. "What herb is this?"

"You ought to ask: what herbs, for there are several. They grow in dark, damp places, and no one on the surface knows their names. Or ever will."

"I see." She licked her lips and sipped the brew. It tasted even better than it smelled—tangy as dill, but with a peppery undertone. "It's nice," she offered between sips. "Do you happen to have food? I haven't eaten since this morning."

"Alas, not enough to fill you. But tomorrow we shall venture to a place where you can gorge." He smiled as she set the pot down. "Rest now."

Her eyes closed, and she listened to his small bustlings. Her heart had calmed, and she breathed normally again. Her problems seemed less formidable after she had been pulled from the brink. And now she had a guide. Yes, it was better to think of him that way. Without a traveling companion from this world, she might find herself in an even worse situation than the one she had just faced. She should ask him a few questions…

The sounds around her quieted, and her thoughts scattered. Her head felt strange…weightless, and sort of stretched. Light glimmered, though her eyes were closed.

A familiar voice spoke, but at a distance. She knew that voice…

"Nya."

Nya crossed the shadowy dining hall to her father, who stood at the hearth, jabbing a poker at some glowing coals. A full bottle of vodka sat on the mantle next to an empty. She took the poker from him and set it in its rack. After a long silence, she said, "Tell me what happened."

"You should be asleep in your bed."

"I won't sleep again until I know."

"Then you won't sleep at all."

She stamped her foot. "I deserve to know how she died! You said it was an accident on the road. But how did it happen, and who was involved?"

He uncapped the vodka and took a long swig. "You deserve not *to know."*

"I will *know. One way or another. She was my mother…" She swallowed back tears. "It's my right!"*

He set the bottle down, a little shakily. "Nothing matters now anyway, does it, poppet? It's over. Everything…"

"Yes. I suppose it is."

He told her.

***

Nya came to slowly, her head spinning. She opened her eyes to darkness. If it weren't for the breeze trickling in through the tunnel door, she would have felt entombed. She sat up a little. "Nenad!"

A soft sound emanated from the back wall, "Yes, my sweet?"

"You drugged me."

"True, true. But you were in no shape to treat your injuries, and you wouldn't have let me treat them, so I did what I had to. If I had not, your wounds would have festered."

Nya's eyes widened in horror at his confession. Gingerly, she patted her middle. The lumps of poultices stood up on her belly, secured with some sort of sticky cloth. "How—"

"I couldn't remove your garments, so I went under them. It was hard work, but I managed it." After a pause, he added, "I also washed the urine off your legs."

Nya dragged her hands over her eyes, then flinched at the bandaging on one palm. She felt sickened, violated. Her voice shook as she growled, "*Never* do anything like that again. Do you understand? I'm not your goat or cow, and my promise only goes as far as it would take me to pitch you over the edge."

He made a clucking sound with his tongue. "I save her life, bandage her wounds, and this is what I get."

"You did those things for selfish reasons."

"Everything we do is for selfish reasons, silly human."

Not true, she thought. Yaro did many small, kind things without expecting anything in return.

"Now go back to sleep," he went on. "It will be a long day tomorrow."

She lay back down with a grunt. She wanted to smash him against the wall, but of course she would not. She ran her hands idly over the poultices, wondering what herbs he had used. She was greedy for them all. Maybe she should ransack his little hole before they left. She had the power to do it, and he deserved to feel the violation he had inflicted on her.

She sighed and closed her eyes. No, just because she could do it didn't make it right. *You can't fight a wrong with another wrong,* her father used to say, and he had been right. He had been right about many things. She pushed aside the memory she had relived and tried to sleep.

The morning light stole in through the open door; with it came hunger. She still lay on the hard floor, sore in multiple places. She didn't realize Nenad was up until fire flared in his tiny lamp. Without a word, he set about packing his things. His clawed fingers dipped into the clay jars, seizing food, herbs, and numerous other small items and storing them in hard leather boxes and pouches. These were in turn tucked away into a well-used sack. When he was finished, he smothered the lamp and gestured toward the tunnel door. "After you."

Once more, she stifled the urge to swat him. *Best to let him think he's got me by the nose,* she thought. At least for a while. Wincing at her stiff foot, she crawled out of the cave and limped up the stairs that climbed the rock wall.

He spoke as he scurried behind her. "The wounds on your belly were made by a rhuksie. What did you do to anger her?"

So the giant birds were known as rhuksies. Nya paused, digging her hand into grooves in the wall. She refused to look over the edge. "I took her robe."

The scurrying ceased. "Sweet Mother," he hissed.

"I didn't know it was hers." She took a slow step. "What happens now?"

"Hopefully, nothing. Once she changes back, she will probably forget you. It's part of their curse, to forget."

"And if she doesn't?"

He made no reply, and neither spoke again until they stood on the short grass that grew near the fissure's edge. Without warning, Nenad leapt onto her leg and climbed her like a cat. "We will move faster if I sit on your shoulder," he said, his warm breath tickling her ear.

Nya's hands balled into fists. "Couldn't you have asked me first?"

"Of course, sweet Nya. But then I wouldn't have had the privilege of feeling the heat of your anger." He grasped one of her braids in his clawed hands and shifted closer to her face.

She asked through clenched teeth, "Where do we go?"

His arm brushed her temple. "Toward that dark rise in the distance."

The sun had barely risen in the overcast sky, but the wind had picked up, finding every place on her clothing that had not fully dried. At least her boots weren't wet. She limped heavily at first, but as her foot heated, it grew more flexible and she found she could ignore the pain.

From a distance, the rise looked like any other ridge in the grassy landscape, but as she neared its top, a different vista opened before her. Nenad was silent as she paused and stared at it.

The remains of a riverbed lay in a hollow in the ridge. Bits of driftwood had been pushed up against the banks, and the bed itself was little more than a long pool of thick mud. She cleared her throat. "How deep is that sludge?"

"I'm not sure, but have no fear. You won't have to cross it."

"Then why are we—"

"Just head down there. I'll tell you when we reach the bottom."

It was no easy feat to descend a driftwood-littered hill with a bad foot, and before long she was on her bottom, half sliding down the slope. Nenad clung to her hair like a burr, making no sound to indicate discomfort. When she was only a yard from the sludge, an old log slowed her momentum, allowing her to stand and recover herself.

It was an odd place. Despite the stench of rot, there were few flies, and the muck dimpled here and there as if full of trapped fish in need of air. Did Nenad expect her to dig for clams? She had never done so, but her rumbling belly told her she would learn if she had to. "What am I to do?" she asked.

"Get closer."

After removing her boots and knotting her skirt up around her waist, she clambered over the log and crouched at the edge of the muck. Nenad clung to her still, his small claws buried in her braids. A breathy sound filled the humid air. In a moment, she knew its source: each dimple in the water contained a brown mouth opening and closing as if drinking the air.

"What are they?" she asked.

"Mudgumps. You've never seen them before?"

"No. And I'm not sure I want to."

"They are delicious when cooked. Many people grow them for food."

At the mention of food, her stomach growled again. "What do I do?" she repeated.

He told her to reach into the mud under a sucking mouth and grasp the gump's neck. "Do it quickly and firmly, or you'll lose him," he warned.

Nya rolled back her sleeve. Her bare feet sank into the warm muck as she waded into the pool. Nenad shifted to her back and went still, waiting.

Quick as a snake, she reached in and grasped the squishy thing beneath the surface. At once, it began to wriggle out of her grip.

"Pull it out!" Nenad squealed.

The mouth opened wider, and rancid air spewed out. Grimacing, she dug her nails deep into its neck and heaved until she leaned back with the effort. At last, there came a horrid sucking sound. Air bubbles burst on the mud's surface, and a bulbous sac emerged under her hands, wriggling this way and that. Nenad scurried down her arm and slashed it with his claw. In response, a brownish red liquid gurgled out, deflating the gump. The creature was perhaps ten inches long and resembled an empty skin bottle.

Her nose wrinkled. "What do I do with this?" Thankfully, it had ceased twitching.

"Set it on the log and clear a spot on the slope for a fire."

Once more, she obeyed him, and before long, they crouched beside a healthy fire, Nya turning the skewered meat. It cooked swiftly, the mud-encrusted skin peeling away to reveal pink meat underneath it.

It was shockingly good. "Like tender, buttery scallops," she murmured between bites. The moment she finished it, she sprang up and seized another wriggling gump, and then another and another until they were stacked on the log like folded undergarments.

After she and Nenad had eaten their fill, he drew a string out of his sack and told her to truss together the necks of the gumps' they hadn't eaten and secure them to her belt for later.

Nya merely nodded, her gaze lingering on the fire's dying flames. They both sat on the log, Nenad with crossed legs. After a time, she asked in a carefully casual tone, "Do you hear a high-pitched sound in the air?"

He tilted his head. "Ah, yes. It started up yesterday, and since then I have stopped listening. Does it bother you, sweet Nya?"

She began trussing the gumps with the string he had set on her lap. The activity made it easier for her to control her mounting eagerness at the conversation. "I don't know how *you* aren't bothered. If a strange sound started up in my world, it's all that people would talk about."

He shrugged his tiny shoulders. "Many strange things come and go here; strange sights, strange sounds, strange smells—" he paused and looked her up and down "—and even strange people." Opening his arms wide, he intoned, "May the Fabric never rest, nor its weave loosen. May we all find peace in the warp and weft of the world."

He spoke the phrases as if they were part of some ancient, well-known prayer.

Nya offered a respectful nod, then spoke once more with deliberate casualness. "So the high-pitched sound emanates from *this* world."

"It does, of course. Everything you see and hear in this world emanates from this world. May the blessed weave never loosen."

Nya let out a long breath and leaned back, leaving the gumps resting on her lap. It was good to finally have an answer, even if it wasn't the one she had hoped for. "I thought so too," she said, "but I wanted to be sure. You see, I know the man making that sound, and I have to find him and help him back to our world."

A troubled look flitted across Nenad's face. Nya pressed her lips together to keep from smiling. The tricky little elf must regret telling her that the windsong emanated from this world. Too late now. "So," she went on, "that is the first thing I must do."

"But you promised!" He beat his fists against his thighs. "You promised, you promised, you—"

"I did. But my promise didn't include a deadline. Help me find him, and I'll do as you ask."

Nenad pushed his chin into his folded arms and huffed. After a minute or two, he spluttered, "He could be anywhere."

So, she thought, could a lake of milk. "I know. That's why I need your help."

"Swear on your name that you'll find the lake. I shan't help you unless you do." He stared her hard in the eyes.

There's power in a name, the lion-girl had said. What exactly did that mean? Would she find herself spiritually bound to complete this task? Or was it merely superstition?

She flung it all to the wind. "I, Nya Stary, swear on my name to find the lake of milk—*after* I help my friend."

There. It was done. And perhaps for the best. Her life was in shambles anyway, and there were worse fates than wandering another world in search of a lake of human milk. A giggle of despair burst from her lips.

When her mouth was still again, she cast a sheepish glance at Nenad, expecting his censure, but his eyes had turned inward, and he seemed lost in thought. At last, he shook himself and looked at her. "You will have to see the griffin," he said, then added, "Or rather, the griffin will have to see you."

CHAPTER SIX

"What is the griffin, and why do I need him?" Nya asked the little man on her shoulder.

He had directed her along the shore until the pool narrowed enough for her to leap over it. Once she had mounted the opposite ridge, Nenad pointed her to a distant line of trees. Something shadowy leaned over it—another ridge perhaps, or a mountain range.

"There is only one left in the world," Nenad said, "and he is ancient beyond telling. He lies curled in a cave in the Grom Mountains. You must open one of his eyelids and ask him what he sees. If he judges you a good person, he shall tell you the truth. It is his curse to do so."

Nya halted. "How would that help me?"

"Because the griffin sees what you cannot see but *need* to see."

"That sounds like a riddle." She chewed her lip. "What happens if he *doesn't* judge me a good person?"

"Don't trouble yourself with that. I wouldn't take you to him if I thought otherwise."

Nya sighed and resumed walking. Life had taught her that few people were entirely good or evil, and the judgement often depended on the one judging. The rhuksie had condemned Nya merely for borrowing a cloak. What would the griffin hold to be important?

She said, "Maybe we should set aside this idea and look for the wind river. I was told that it might lead to a Windsinger."

"Whoever told you that wished you dead. Wind rivers are perilous."

"Seems like everything is here."

"Only the things *you* choose to do."

"That's not fair. I didn't choose to be plucked up by a rhuksie and dropped into a crevice."

He let out a breathy chuckle. "No, I suppose not." He leaned his head against her cheek. "Sweet Nya, I wouldn't suggest you see the griffin if I thought he would hurt you. So humor me. If this idea fails, we shall move on to another."

She gave a reluctant nod, and they both fell silent. Nya stopped at a thin stream to wash her face and quench her thirst, then on they went toward the deepening wall of darkness that spread across the horizon—the home of the griffin. Nenad wouldn't let her dwell on it but broke into several lengthy chants about the Fabric and one about the Lake Lady. His warm breath tickled her ear, and more than once she had to suppress the urge to swat him away. At least he distracted her from the painful thoughts she was tempted to gnaw on. Goran's betrayal loomed over her like a physical presence. In some ways, it was even worse than his death. It made her want to dissect every conversation they'd had, every look. Not even her father escaped the web Goran had spun. Had Adrion known in advance that Goran wanted that property, and if so, had he known why?

She swallowed sharply and shook her head. It was too awful to contemplate.

The only thing that mattered now was Yaro. He didn't deserve to be trapped in this world, especially not for repairing the damage her brother had caused. She tried to pick his windsinging out of Nenad's harassing lines. There was something... Suddenly, she gasped and looked up at the low clouds that had blown in.

"What is it?" Nenad cooed.

"A rhuksie. I'm sure I heard one."

Just then, a dark shape scudded through the clouds above them.

"Run," Nenad hissed.

The dense forest at the base of the mountain was still a hundred yards off. If the rhuksie was determined to catch them, they didn't stand a chance. "If it's not after me, running might draw its attention," she said as she quickened her pace.

An unearthly shriek split the air.

"It's circling." Nenad's voice shook, and his claws bit into her scalp.

Nya ran. The rhuksie screamed above her, louder this time and throatier, as if the woman in it was bellowing in anger. Could it be the same one? She forced herself to move faster, even as the meadow thickened with ferns and sticky vines. The instant she heard the thud of massive wings, a wind river leapt into her path, moving so fast that the grass under it was bent almost flat. Unable to stop in time, she jumped onto it and rolled. Talons raked her leg, and a wing pinned her to the river. Another cry pierced her ears, then the wing lifted and there came a scramble of feathers and claws. All of a sudden, the rhuksie tumbled off the wind river and hopped away.

"Nenad?" Nya touched her head and felt the wetness of blood.

The little man wriggled out from under her shoulder. "I'm fine, just a little bruised. Where is the rhuksie?"

"Behind us somewhere. I think the river injured it."

Nenad clambered onto her back. "Sweet Lady of the Lake," he whispered.

The forest sped by. The wind river was faster than it had been the day before. The ferns beneath it looked like seaweed wrenched in a current. Nya struggled to her feet, wincing at the pain that lanced her leg. Blood streamed from the new wounds, some of it seeping into her boot. The old wounds throbbed, and some must have broken open, for her belly felt warm and sticky with fluid. Just then, she spied a path through the dense woods. She pointed it out to Nenad as it flashed by.

"That is a wind path," he muttered. "Made long ago by a fierce wind river. Nya, you must—"

"Jump. I know. Hang on!" Fists clenched, she leapt into an approaching fern. She tried to land on her feet, but the river's momentum made her tumble and roll. Weeds as tough as cords bit into her injuries. She whimpered as she rolled onto her back and struggled to rise.

Nenad, who had come off her at some point, stood on the crushed, bloodied ferns as if they were a podium. "Up!" he urged. "Now! Let's go."

"The blood—I need to bandage my leg."

"No time!"

Was the rhuksie after them again? Her heart juddered as she forced herself to stand and run. Nenad scurried ahead, his small sack bouncing on his back. They tore through the ferns and scaled jutting rocks until trees loomed over them, their heavy, crooked bows casting deep shadows on the ground. Nya slowed, feeling faint. "We need to find that wind path."

"Not now, it's too open. Can you climb that rocky outcrop? We can rest on the other side of it."

Nya followed his pointed finger to some crags at the top of a low rise. If she had not been injured, she might have scaled it in a few minutes. As it was… "I'll try."

Limping, she dragged herself up the hill, grasping fistfuls of ferns as she went. She slipped on the mossy rocks and almost fell, but her good leg held her, and, shaking, she managed to haul herself over the ledge and into a sort of cave on the other side. Darkness enveloped her then, a lovely, welcoming night…

"Nya! You must stay awake."

She heard a cutting sound, like a knife tearing through fabric. Nenad wriggled under her legs, and the sound ceased. She blinked to keep her eyes open.

"Sit up, Nya."

"Can't."

"You can and you will. You'll do it for your friend."

"Bastard."

"I've been called worse."

"I can think of worse." She groaned as she forced herself to a sitting position.

Nenad stood by a hill of cloth that he had doubtless sheared off the bottom of her skirt. He flicked a bit of lint from his claw. "Your bandage, my sweet. And here are the herbs for a poultice. Use them sparingly." He held out a tiny leather box. A green salve lay inside it, warmed from sitting in the sack against his back.

The rest of the day passed in a painful blur. After she had bandaged her leg, Nenad opened another box and passed it to her without a word. She knew by the smell what nameless herbs lay inside it and what he wished to do, but she ate them anyway and woke from her drugged state to find her belly cleaned and the poultices changed. Her eyes closed.

When she opened them again, warmth grazed her face. Night had fallen. Nenad sat cross-legged beside a small fire, his clawed fingers picking apart a mudgump. "You should eat some," he said when he noticed her watching him. "They won't keep,"

"I thought they came off the string when the bird attacked."

"A few did. Only these four remain." He waved to a stack at his side.

Nya's mouth was dry, but she forced herself to chew and swallow the pieces he offered her, and afterward she felt better for it.

She leaned against the rock wall and studied the stars she could glimpse through the branches overhead. Could they be the same as the ones in her world? The idea was vaguely comforting. "Thank you," she said.

"For what?"

"For dressing my wounds, for the food. I know why you help me, but I appreciate it all the same."

He stood and bowed. "My pleasure, sweet Nya."

Her eyes were threatening to close. She swallowed back a stickiness in her throat. "Wish we had water."

Nenad's strange, high voice seemed to slip out of the whistling wood. "A small stream trickles down from the mountain. We shall encounter it on the way to the griffin tomorrow."

The griffin. She sighed and closed her eyes. "How do you know where all these things are—the griffin, the water…?"

"The chima recorded them in maps during their travels. My people possess those maps now. They are a great treasure."

If he said more, Nya didn't hear it.

She woke to dappled sunlight on her face. Nenad was already up and ready to go. Nya choked down the last of the mudgumps and then forced herself to stand. Her body was stiff and painful, but thirst drove her to put one sore foot in front of the other. She moved so slowly that Nenad ran ahead, returning to tell her which ways were easiest. The mountain's slope was gentle at first, but as the trees gave way to stone, it steepened, and the narrow walkways Nenad found for her were treacherous.

When they finally found a stream, Nya could not spare her hands to drink. Instead, she gripped the mossy rock wall, straddling the pool in her path, and sipped water as it fell from some fantastic height above. She was wet and cold by the time she had quenched her thirst. She could have borne such discomforts with ease if it weren't for her injuries, but the dampness woke every pain in her body.

"Just a little farther," Nenad said tightly.

Around a bend, the rock wall steepened to a sheer cliff that curved in like a horseshoe. Mist hung in the curve, concealing the ledge she was using as a path. A smudge of darkness lay behind that mist. "Is it the cave?" she whispered.

For once, Nenad seemed unable to speak. His former confidence had melted away, leaving a wild-eyed, frozen statue that would have frightened children in a garden.

"Nenad, are we doing this or not?"

His chest moved as he drew a sharp breath. "You should go in alone."

"Why? Are you afraid of the griffin?"

He gave no answer. Nya cleared her throat and wiped sweat from her eyes. "I don't know what makes you so sure he'll accept me. *You* don't even know me."

"I don't have to. If you were evil, I would know it."

She shook her head but judged it useless to say more. "Will I have to travel far in the cave? Should I bring your little lamp?"

"No, it is high noon, and the beast is close to the entrance. Stay here. I'll scout the path for you."

He disappeared into the mist. Moments later, he returned to say the ledge was safe. Nya had her doubts, but she pushed them aside and edged along the path.

The world turned white and silent. Even Yaro's windsinging faded until it sounded only in her mind. At last, her groping hands found the cave edge, and she limped inside. As she made her way up an almost smooth incline, the mist thinned, allowing her to see the massive cave she had entered. The walls on either side had to be a hundred feet apart, the edges decorated by a prickly array of stalactites. All was still but for an intermittent dripping.

The incline leveled, and a layer of moss swept over the floor like a foamy wave. She winced as her boots sank into it, but at least it dampened her footsteps. She was beginning to make out the back wall now. Unlike the cave's steep sides, it looked to be a jumble of boulders, some painted green with moss. The mist eddied strangely at one end. Perhaps there was a small opening that allowed air in.

She slowed and stared at the shifting mist, prickles creeping up her back and neck. There was a pattern to the eddying, much like breathing. But it couldn't be. No creature was large enough to displace that much air.

Her eyes traveled once more over the boulders, and this time she made out the suggestion of a wing, a folded paw, a curled talon. And behind the eddying mist, a massive beak, all of it peppered with moss.

She could not move. Her hands, tucked under her folded arms, were deadened chunks of ice. Her legs were weak, wobbling things. What if Nenad was wrong? Everyone knew it wasn't wise to wake a large, slumbering animal.

But this was no cave bear, and by the look of the moss, it had been curled this way for some time. How fast could a creature move after mouldering in one spot for so long? She forced herself to take a step. Open an eyelid, Nenad had said. Just one.

She thought she could smell the beast now—a sweet, musty scent like that of old honey in a cellar. When the warmth of its breath grazed her legs, she almost bolted. Instead, she dropped to the floor and crawled through the shifting mist to its enormous head. The beak alone was as long as her body. Moss spilled over its folded lion ears and down its feathered forehead. Half its face was cushioned in its paw so that only one lidded eye was visible. Nya stretched out a trembling hand and touched its leathery upper lid. No response. Kneeling by the beak, she shoved her fingers into the crack between its upper and lower lids and pulled hard. The crack widened, and then some white, filmy lid underneath slid aside. The eye flashed open.

Nya jerked her hands back but could not obey the urge to retreat. She sat in a warm pool of the griffin's breath, pinned by his round yellow eye. Not since she had stared into the Witterkin had she felt so stunned.

A universe lay in that aged, intelligent gaze. She felt herself sinking down into a deep bow.

At last, the griffin spoke, his red tongue moving in his curved beak. "Crystal Mountain," he rumbled, and then the white lid slid across and the outer lids closed over it. To Nya, it felt like a door closing.

She stumbled and righted herself. "Is that all, wise one?"

No answer. Surely he could hear her. She drew closer to his ear. "Talk to me. Please. I'm in need of your wisdom." She ran her hand down his mossy beak, considered opening his eye again, and decided against it. She didn't want to tempt his anger. Instead, she sat back down in the warmth of his breath and told him her tale.

The mists thinned, and frail sunlight fanned into the cave. She had long finished speaking when Nenad's voice came to her from the entrance, sounding for all the world like a bird cry.

"I'm coming," she called back dejectedly.

The little chima stood trembling at the cave's entrance. "What happened?"

"He spoke to me." She limped past him toward the ledge.

"Is that all? What did he say?"

"I can't talk now. Too tired." Her voice sounded rough and weak to her ears. She leaned heavily against the rock wall as she walked, favoring her uninjured foot. Her activities in the cave must have jostled her injuries, for they throbbed something terrible.

Neither of them spoke again until they returned to the ridge where they had spent the night. Nya collapsed against the rock then, every part of her aching. She stared bleakly through the branches toward the rock shelves beyond. "We weren't as high up as I thought," she murmured.

She must have fallen asleep, for when she opened her eyes again it was dark and Nenad was crouched beside his little fire.

"I gathered some berries and edible mushrooms," he said when she shuffled closer to him.

Nya picked a blueberry off the top of a foot-high hill of foraged food. "You must have been at it all evening."

He waved his hand. "I had nothing better to do. Eat."

"I will. With thanks."

She scooped up a handful and ate quickly and self-consciously. She hated to admit it, but she had gone from resenting him to feeling vaguely guilty. How long would he work to nourish her before realizing she couldn't bring him to his fabled lake?

He had even cleaned the mushrooms for her.

"Can you talk now?" Nenad asked when she was well into the pile.

She gave a faint nod. "'Crystal Mountain.' That's what he said."

Nenad looked at her sharply, his eyes wide. He spoke as if he wasn't sure he had heard her right. "Crystal Mountain."

"Yes. What does it mean?"

He stabbed a twig into the fire. "It might mean you've attracted some unwanted attention."

"The attention of whom?"

"You'll see."

Her brow furrowed. "What do you mean, I'll see? Are you saying I'll have to go to this place?" She did not relish another mountain climb.

He shrugged and looked away from her searching eyes. "You shall go there, whether you wish to or not. The griffin saw it in your path."

Nya bristled. "I don't *have* to do anything. I have control over my own fate. If I wanted to, I could go back to the Witterkin and throw myself into them."

"You could, but you won't. There are many paths to take, but we never leave the warp to join the weft."

Nya snatched up another handful of berries and ate to keep from speaking. While she did not believe in fate, there were other ways to view the griffin's message. If he truly possessed the ability to see into someone, then he might also view their future, including all the branching paths. Was it possible he had chosen one for her as the best course to take? If so, she ought to heed his advice. "All right." She rubbed her sticky hands on the rock wall. "Say I go to Crystal Mountain. Will what I find there be dangerous?"

"No. But the journey to it *is*. We can follow the forest for a time, but we'll eventually have to leave it and enter the open grassland."

"The rhuksie," she muttered.

"Yes."

She leaned against the rock wall with a sigh. "Well we can't stay in the forest forever. How high is the mountain?"

"Many times higher than the griffin's cave. But there are stairs going up it."

"Stairs. What kind of place is it?"

"It is a mountain of crystal. Go back to sleep, Nya. And don't be troubled by your path." He began to sing softly about the Fabric. Warp and weft, spindle and loom…

Such an odd creature, she thought.

As she drifted between sleep and waking, the image of a wooden beam formed in her mind, like those used for ships' masts. Bright threads glistened over it, shuddering as they rose and fell. A thousand threads. More. And the machinery she could *not* see creaked and thudded but never stopped moving…

She woke while it was still dark and stared at the remains of the fire. Crickets chirred, a night bird called, and somewhere Yaro played on, his song like a net spread over the world. Her throat closed as she listened to it. There was no mistaking his unique style. But where was he? How could he be in a single location if the overall volume of his windsinging never varied?

She was afraid of the answer. She would rather wander this place forever than find Yaro dead, or worse, alive but unable to break free of whatever evil held him. What would she do if she couldn't help him?

She shoved the thought away and tried to sleep. Her injured body needed time to heal.

The next morning was damp and chill. She and Nenad spoke little as they left the cave and climbed down the ridge to the forest's edge. They traveled just inside the edge, where the sparse undergrowth allowed them to travel separately but still concealed from rhuksies. Nya's habit of eying the ground for herbs as she walked served her well, for she uncovered a tiny stream, almost hidden by ferns and vine.

As she stooped to drink, a familiar yellow-leafed plant peeked at her through the ferns.

"I know you," she whispered, tipping it toward her. "And look at all your seeds." She broke off a branch and tucked it into her battered pouch.

The water took the edge off her hunger, and she was able to hobble behind Nenad until early afternoon. He turned them back into the forest then, promising food, and sure enough, at the base of a rock wall where the land scooped down, another mud hole lay. Nya rushed to it without a word and heaved out as many gumps as she could reach. Meanwhile, Nenad built a fire and found a spit.

There was comfort in a full belly. Problems fell away, and the future seemed less bleak. Nya wiped her greasy hands on the weedy ground and grinned at Nenad across the fire. "Your sack reminds me of a pillowcase."

"That, my sweet Nya, is because it is one. This is my conception pillowcase."

She blinked. "Your what?"

"Why, the case upon which my mother's head rested while she and my father—"

"Never mind," she said quickly, her face heating.

She cringed as he patted the stained case. He said, "No chima travels without his conception pillowcase." He drew it closer and laid his head on it. "There is a tale of a chima who lost his case. He was traveling across the lip of a dormant volcano when he stumbled and fell; his case came loose and tumbled into the pit. Loath to go on, he chose to climb down after it. After a month, he returned to his people with stories of diamonds and great spaces in the earth. There is a rich city in that volcano now, all because a chima wouldn't abandon his conception pillowcase."

"Seems foolish to travel along the lip of a volcano, dormant or not."

"That matters not! The point is—"

"Never abandon your conception pillowcase. I know." She grinned, enjoying his bout of temper. After a silence, she asked, "Are your parents still alive?"

"No. My kind only lives to about forty years. I have but two decades left to find my lake." As if reminded by this lack, he stood and brushed the dirt off his sacred pillowcase. "Let us be off."

For two days more, they traveled at the forest's edge. When the sky was free of clouds that might conceal rhuksies, Nenad sang of his Lake Lady, and the steady thumping of the cooked mudgumps against Nya's hip provided an unintended drumbeat. When Nya focused on the land beyond the woods, she glimpsed a distant lake, followed by perhaps a mile of dark bog land. Then fields and ridges again. On the second evening, as twilight fell, Nenad waved her out of the forest and asked what she saw in the open landscape. A bright moon was rising in a hazy violet sky. Somewhere to the right of it lay a huge, faintly gleaming shape. Nya's skin prickled. "I think—hey!"

Nenad's claws bit into her clothing as he climbed to her shoulder. Once there, he went deadly still.

"Well?" she prodded.

"The rhuksies often hunt at night," he whispered.

"But what about *that?*" She pointed at the shape.

"That is the mountain of course. Crystal Mountain." He leaned closer to her ear, and she could swear she felt him shudder. "Do you see how it reflects the moonlight? Just wait until daytime. You will wish you were blind."

They found some boulders in the forest to huddle against and slept without making a fire. The night was warm and sticky, carrying with it biting flies. When Nya couldn't keep them away from her face, she leapt to her feet and ran out of the woods into the weedy field. "Let the rhuksie take me," she shouted at Nenad, who had managed to scramble onto her shoulder before she took off.

"If only we had derefa sap."

"Well, we don't." She stumbled on a rock and righted herself. Tall grass brushed her legs; she sank down into it and curled into a ball. Moments later, raindrops splattered her cheek. Nenad burrowed under her curled leg and went still. Nya had no such comfort. At least the rain kept the flies at bay. Hunching her shoulders, she tried to sleep.

Dawn was another kind of darkness. They rose, damp and shivering, and ate what remained of the mudgumps. The rain had ceased, and heavy winds swept over the plain. The sky was a shadowy, shifting mass of clouds.

The moment they finished breakfast, Nya scooped Nenad up and set him on her shoulder. He did not complain. Neither of them had the energy to speak.

Shivering, she forced herself to a fast walk toward the mountain. Her injuries screamed at her, but she couldn't afford to heed the pain. She needed to get warm, and she didn't like the long, open space that stretched before her. After days of walking under trees, she felt exposed, a wounded animal with no weapon or shelter.

"Some say that rhuksies don't hunt in strong winds," Nenad said.

"And some say that evil can become a beast. Doesn't make it so."

"I wonder if rhuksies are such beasts..."

"If that were true, we wouldn't stand a chance."

A hole had opened in the boot of her good foot, letting in muddy water. She had thread in her pouch, but it wasn't strong enough for boot leather. She thought about wrapping the toe with material from her skirt but couldn't bring herself to pause.

The mountain was farther away than it looked, and she found herself eyeing the ground to avoid becoming frustrated by her seeming lack of progress. She had walked for years, it seemed. Centuries. Her bad foot ached, and her calves were red with small scratches. But at last she drew near to the mountain's foot.

It was a fortress of a mountain, made from towers of crystal that jutted every which way. Under the overcast sky, they looked like shards of ice. She shivered and folded her arms. "Where are the stairs?"

"They begin on the mountain's east side, so…" She felt him shift on her shoulder. "They will be more to the right."

She corrected her course and trudged on, her focus on the mountain this time. She imagined it would be beautiful in the sunlight, the glittering crystals scattering color. Probably a good thing for her eyes that it was overcast.

"Best to keep your eyes down," Nenad muttered.

"It isn't overly bright."

"I know. But there are other reasons to examine the ground."

Nya, too weary to argue, bent her head and watched where she placed her feet. Minutes later, dirty chunks of crystal appeared, some lying as if thrown, others jutting from deep in the earth. She felt oddly reluctant to tread on them. Even without sunlight, something stirred deep in their depths, like a memory of light, trapped and curling within.

Movement in her peripheral vision made her glance up, but she saw nothing, only more crystal.

"They are not poisonous," Nenad murmured.

"What aren't?"

"The mountain snakes."

She slowed, her eyes widening. "Where? Are you talking about the coiling light within the crystals?"

As Nenad began to answer, a real snake slithered in the weeds near her foot. Hastily, she danced away, almost falling in the process. "Those are real," she gasped.

"Of course. Sadly, we cannot eat them. It is prohibited."

"Why would we want to?"

"Why wouldn't we? Snake is delicious. When cooked, of course."

Somehow, it didn't surprise her that Nenad enjoyed snake. She paused and examined the ground. One slithered up and over a squat chunk of crystal. As it did so, it changed from dull brown to a deep shiny red. The bright color lasted as long as the snake touched the crystal, then it returned to dull brown. Nya stooped, careful not to jostle Nenad, and seized a shard. Right away, her hand blurred and changed. Her fingers became long and elegant; her nails lost their roughness and curved into perfect ovals. She lifted her other hand and observed the same effect. "Incredible," she whispered. "And I didn't feel a thing. Does my face look different?"

Nenad sucked in a sharp breath. "You can see the change?"

"Yes. Why? Is that bad?"

"No, but...I've always been told that humans are unable to see it." There was a note of worry in his voice. Perhaps he feared she was not human after all and thus could not guide him to his treasured lake of milk.

She tossed the crystal away and resumed walking. "How do your people know that?"

"Because humans have passed through this world over the centuries. Their visits are rare, but they happen."

Nya's grandmother popped into her mind. As a young woman, she had been dragged out of the Witterkin, stunned and unable to recall her own name. And because she had been a stranger, talk was that she had come from "the land of the good folk." Nya had always scoffed at the idea. Now, she wondered if there wasn't a grain of truth to the tale. Her grandmother had been human, of course, but perhaps one of those rare humans who had traveled to another world. "When was the last time a human came here?" she asked.

"I don't know," he admitted. "My people only remember the humans who've had dealings with chima. Those encounters are recorded as tales."

"I'd like to hear those tales."

He was silent a moment and then said haltingly, "Are you certain that you are…?"

"I am human, Nenad. You can rest your mind about that."

The rain returned then, the heavy drops chasing the snakes into their hidey-holes. Nya hunched her shoulders and trudged on, watching the ground as Nenad had suggested. As she drew closer to the mountain, Nenad flicked his arm against her temple. "There. Do you see the steps?"

She lifted her head, and blinking away raindrops, glimpsed a winding line on the slope.

His arm brushed her again. "And there—look, a path to it."

Nya had no energy to respond. The strength she had possessed in the meadow had long worn off, but she refused to stop, even on the mountain.

Especially not on the mountain. Birds of prey had keen eyes, and there were no trees on the slope. Nya would be as good as offering herself to the rhuksie.

"What was that, Nya? You muttered something..."

"Nothing." She veered toward the path, weaving around jutting stones. The crystals were becoming larger and more plentiful the nearer she came to the slope. Soon, she would have no space to plant her feet. Some of the crystals looked sharp enough to cut through the soles of her boots.

Nenad said, "Do not fear your path in the Fabric. It might seem—"

Nya flung her hand back and grabbed his head. "Enough about the Fabric!" She let go, and he shrank down against her neck.

Finally, she reached the path, which was built from slabs of cut crystal, roughened in some way to create a tread. Where, she wondered, were all the people who had cut this stone? So far, she had seen no sign that anyone lived on the mountain. No guards or gates. If it weren't for the griffin, she would have turned back.

Nenad remained stiffly silent. He was probably putting on a show of being hurt so that she would apologize. Well, she wasn't about to be toyed with that way. He had to learn that he was not Nya's master, even if the lesson hurt both of them.

The stairs that wound around the mountain were wider than they had looked from a distance and appeared to have been cut from the mountain, rather than placed. All were properly horizontal, with no cracks or wear to speak of. A sad smile tugged on her lips. How Yaro would have loved this masonry! He would have spent days up here, trying to divine how the steps had been cut. The fact that crystal was different from windstone wouldn't have mattered.

She sighed, and her steps grew heavier. Thinking about Yaro made her mind veer into places it should not. The sweetness was always ruined by bitterness—not that that had kept her from thinking about him lately. She could almost feel him walking at her side, blocking the wind and rain with his large body. The imagined presence made her heart ache.

She groaned. "All right, Nenad, you can talk."

"I don't wish to."

Of course not. "Very well."

She forced herself to clear her mind and move on, wincing at the pain it cost her. Time slowed to sludge, like the stuff the mudgumps lived in. If only she had caught and cooked more. Hunger was gnawing a hole in her belly. She spied a depression in a broken chunk of crystal and paused to sip the rainwater from it. Her hand transformed as she grazed the crystal with her bare skin. She glanced sideways at Nenad. "Does the crystal only change my hands, or—"

"It changes your whole body." He crawled down her arm and laid his palm on the wet rock. At once, his features smoothed and somehow became more symmetrical. Had his nose been crooked before? In any case, it was straight now, and his chin looked more defined. His other features were too small for Nya to make out well with her tired eyes.

"You should rest," Nenad said.

"If I do, I'll never move again."

"If you don't, you will drop where you stand. Sit down, sit down, sit down…"

She ignored his screeching chant and pushed on. About halfway up the mountain, the stairs disappeared for several yards under what looked to be an avalanche of broken crystals. The shape of the stairs was still there, but climbing on the shards would be perilous.

"Don't move!" Nenad scrambled down her body and rushed into her path, opening his arms.

"I wasn't about to walk on that. But what now? There's no way around them." She peered over the edge. On one side was the drop, on the other a sheer wall of large crystals.

"We clear a space," he said. "Tear another strip off your skirt and wrap your hands so they won't be cut."

Soon she wouldn't have a skirt. She did as he asked and then, beginning where the debris was thinnest, tugged out chunks of heavy crystal and cast them aside, wincing at the clatter. As soon as a step peeked out, she thrust her foot onto it. And then another. At times, small shards trickled down into the space she had created, forcing her to clear it again. Nenad worked with her until a chunk of crystal knocked him over. Nya placed him back on her shoulder and went on working. She had only a few more feet to clear when she lost her footing and fell forward. Wet crystals slid under her palms, their edges biting her skin. As she began to slide back, a white panic gripped her heart. Ignoring her wounds, she clambered on her hands and knees over the shards until she reached the clean stairs on the other side. Trembling, she lowered herself down on a step, leaned her head against the slope, and closed her eyes.

Nenad unstuck his claws from her braids and touched her knee. "You're hurt."

She opened her eyes a crack, saw blood, and closed them. Nenad tugged gently on her skirt, and there came a ripping sound. Nya dropped her leg a little so he could remove crystal shards and bind the wounds. And then the other leg. And then her forearm. He used the wrappings around her palms to secure the bandages.

By the time he was finished, the step was red with her blood.

"It's not so bad," he assured her, his shaky voice betraying his words. "As for the blood on the step, half of it's rainwater."

She did not reply. The rain and wind had let up, opening a small bubble of calm. Nya drifted into it.

She woke shivering. Folding her arms only made her colder. She rose with an effort and trudged up the stairs again, her wet boots thudding on the crystal. Nenad scrambled after her. "Nya, wait!"

She paused long enough to allow him to climb her, then trudged on. This time, though, she allowed herself rest stops. If the rhuksie came for her, it wouldn't matter whether Nya was on the mountain's slope or its peak. She would be done for either way.

She was about to rest again when Nenad whispered, "We're here. We have reached the top."

"What?" She straightened her hunched shoulders and looked up. Sure enough, the stairs ended only a few yards away. Two crystal pillars stood like sentinels on either side of the landing. As she climbed, she glimpsed others, none of them taller than an average-sized man, but together they formed a loose ring around the summit, perhaps intending to conceal what lay within from those who looked up from below. The summit itself looked to be about a hundred feet across.

She passed between the pillars and halted.

A crystal path stretched from the stairs to a ring of black megaliths. Within the stone circle, the ground was smooth, as if polished by fire. Outside it was a sea of jagged, unworked crystal. Nya cleared her raw throat. "There's no one here."

"Keep going," Nenad said.

"Very well." Her skin prickled as she neared the ring of standing stones. Its center was not merely smooth, but clear, like a transparent layer of ice on a still lake, baring fathomless depths below.

The mountain's center was pure, solid crystal.

She stepped onto it and then dropped to the ground in exhaustion. Wind tickled stray hairs against her forehead. The craggy megaliths loomed over her. One had a small gap in it, like a cloudy eye, watching.

"Now what?" she breathed. It seemed right to speak in whispers up here.

"Now we wait, sweet Nya. Or rather, you wait, and I sleep."

"Wait for what?" She lay down, unlatched her pouch, and set it under her head. She may as well be comfortable.

"For what the griffin saw."

CHAPTER SEVEN

Nya hung suspended, in the deepest peace she had ever experienced. Part of that peace had to do with all the many memories she held, each like a bright star in a vast green universe, and all connected through feather-fine threads of awareness. She was so deep, so old. The power in that great age was something felt but never consciously considered. Without disturbance, power was restful, another aspect of what she was.

Peace, silence –

And then a scream. The stars shivered and began to darken. The connections between them severed, each break a small destruction of herself. She tried to salvage power in the remaining connections, but they broke as fast as they flared. Her scream built and became pain, a deep, unbearable agony that echoed through her into her neighboring kin. Their tortured response was the last thing she experienced before blackness closed in, and she knew no more.

Nya awoke panting, her head cradled in her folded arms. "It was my brother, not me, not me," she whimpered into the mountain, for she knew she had dreamt the Witterkin's death. All this time, she had thought only of Goran's death and betrayal. She had not dwelled on the terrible possibility that the Witterkin had thoughts and feelings like people did and had therefore felt themselves dying. It was too awful to contemplate.

"It wasn't you," agreed a female voice from above her.

Nya stiffened in shock and lifted her head. A tall woman stood in the light of a fire, which blazed in a bowl on the ground in the center of the stone circle. A foot-long potato-shaped object hung over the bowl on a metal spit.

The woman smiled. She would have passed for human if it weren't for her overly large eyes and long limbs. Her flowing white robe seemed to glow against her dark skin. As she crouched by the bowl, a black braid slid over one shoulder. "My name is Merima. Are you hungry?"

"I am," Nya said warily. She was curious about all the activity that had happened near her while she slept but was afraid to ask about it. She rose stiffly and looked around her. Night had fallen. Nenad slept against one of the shadowy megaliths. Nya stifled an urge to wake him. He seemed to think she should face this encounter alone, and so she would.

The woman took the spit off the fire and hooked its handle over the lip of the bowl so that the food hung over the floor rather than the flames. "This is called a klooben. It is dense and hearty. People in your world might compare it to a sweet potato."

"How do you know about my world?"

Merima merely smiled. She drew a flask from a pocket in her robe and held it out. "Water."

Nya uncapped it, furtively sniffed its contents and then downed half in a few gulps. The water slid like ice down her parched throat. It took all her self-control not to empty the bottle.

"Keep the rest," Merima offered. "As for the klooben, it will take time to cool. We will use that time to talk." She strode past Nya to one of the dark megaliths. Nya set the bottle down and followed, expecting her to sit on the floor against the stone. Instead, the woman climbed it with a practiced ease and settled, cross-legged, on the top.

And that was when Nya saw the others—eleven more humanoid figures, each perched on a stone, silent and still. She turned slowly, her breath frozen in her throat.

Lamp light flared, and her gaze was tugged toward one of the figures. A man this time, his skin pale and his hair gray and curling. He set his lamp on the stone. "I am Bogdan."

"You give your names so easily," Nya said, not quite controlling the waver in her voice. The weight of twelve pairs of eyes pressed on her now. She was surrounded, with nowhere to go and no friend to support her if she were attacked in some way. She doubted that Nenad would intrude, even if he were awake.

"That is the privilege of power," Bogdan replied. He had a dry, flat voice and over-enunciated his words, like merchants in her world did when talking to foreigners. "We are the Attendants of the Prince of Time. Some call us the Keepers of Fate, or simply the Keepers. But no words in your language can truly describe our purpose, so be satisfied with names. You are Nya."

"Yes..."

"Good. What do you know about the Witterkin?"

Her jaw slackened. After her terrible dream, the question did not feel like a coincidence. "Not much," she managed.

He nodded, as if he had expected that answer. "Then you are in good company. Our knowledge of them is likewise scanty. However, I will share what we know, since it is important that you also know it.

"The Witterkin are the oldest beings in this world. As far as we can tell, they do not age and are not affected by the elements. But this you already know. What you do not know is their purpose: they are the recorders of time. For millennia, they have absorbed and stored events, both great and small. Their memories are perfect and changeless, and for that reason alone, they are important to our prince, and to anyone who appreciates the value of having a knowledge of the past.

"Unfortunately, eight centuries ago a few Witterkin shifted from this world into yours, creating a bridge of sorts. A bridge between worlds." His lips curved in a humorless smile. "And that brings us to your brother. When he poisoned the Witterkin in your world, he triggered a disease, which spread to the Witterkin in ours. The man your people call a Windsinger healed them, thanks be to the gods. If he had not, the red Witterkin would have eventually covered *both* worlds until nothing existed but a red sea." He leaned forward. "Do you understand the seriousness of the situation now?"

"Yaromir."

"What was that?"

Her quavering voice rose. "The Windsinger's name is Yaromir."

Bogdan's lips twitched. "Yaromir," he repeated, nodding. Then to her surprise, he tossed his lamp to a figure perched on the next stone over.

The light revealed a woman with short silver hair, slanted eyes, and a pointed chin. Her head tilted as she observed Nya. There was no warmth in her gaze; it was like being regarded by the moon. "You *do* understand," she said. "But you do not think beyond your present concerns. You say to yourself, 'I regret what happened, but it is over now. They were healed.'" She paused, raising a silver eyebrow. Then she tossed the lamp to another.

"Nya," a dark-skinned man said, his voice a deep baritone, "have you ever heard it said that we must look both ways before taking an important step? You have looked back, and now you must look forward. We are fortunate to have a Windsinger as talented as Yaromir. But one day this disaster will happen again. If Yaromir dies before that day..." His voice trailed off, as if he wished her to finish his thought.

She forced her clenched lips to loosen. "Then let him return to our world so he can train another."

"This is not something that can be learned. It is in the blood and in the heart." He punched a fist to his chest. "He *must* have an heir."

So he was alive and well, or the man wouldn't have said that. Her heart lurched. "He'll have one," she promised recklessly. "Someone will marry him and give him children."

The man shook his head. "He is no longer looking for a wife. You care for him. You must marry him."

There was a silence, broken only by Nenad's squeaky snoring. Nya's face felt hot against the cool air. How could they know so much? Were they bluffing? She tried to gather her frayed thoughts. "You talk about him like he's some breeding horse and not a real person."

The man opened his mouth to answer, then looked to his side as if someone had called his name. He tossed the lamp.

Merima caught it with a graceful flick of her wrist. "What do you know about breeding, Nya?" She paused, and her teeth flashed white against her dark face. "Admit it: you speak out of ignorance. You know nothing of your own mortal magics."

Mortal magics. The words chimed oddly in Nya's ears. She said, "I have no magic."

A rumble of chuckles moved through the circle. Nya turned restlessly, her fists clenched so hard that her nails bit into her palms. A thickness in her throat told her she was on the verge of tears. But why? What was the point of standing here and letting them mock her? She ought to just say yes to whatever they wanted, just as she'd said to Nenad in the crack.

She tried but found she could not. She hugged herself, shivering in the cold mist that had begun to gather. There had been such a mist on the night her father revealed how her mother had died.

Her eyes were hard as she met Merima's again. Perhaps the Keepers didn't know everything. "I *want* to be with him," she admitted, "but I can't."

"And why is that?"

"Because he killed my mother." Her voice cracked.

In her mind, she stood again with her father by the hearth, listening to how it had happened. The spooked horse, the wagon weighed down by windstone, the blood…so much blood. Yet no one but her father and Yaro had been there to witness it. At her father's request, the local watchman had agreed to keep some of the details confidential.

She cleared the tears from her throat and said, "I know it was an accident, and I didn't hold it against him. I still don't, but that doesn't change the fact that it happened. It happened, and now it will always be between us."

There. She had finally spoken the terrible words aloud. She couldn't believe it was to these creatures.

Nenad's snoring had stopped. In the silence, Yaro's windsinging drifted back to her ears, reminding Nya of what she was there to do. She swiped away tears and pleaded, "Help him. Please. If you have any sense of justice at all. He helped you, so help him. Help me find him and bring him home."

Was it a trick of the light, or did Merima look sympathetic? She pursed her lips at Nya. "You never answered Bogdan's question. Do you understand the—?"

"Yes. The Windsinger needs an heir—someone who can heal the Witterkin if my people become greedy."

Merima smiled, evidently pleased with her answer. As she looked past Nya to Bogdan, a strange buzzing filled the air. After a while, Nya realized it was speech. The Keepers were conferring in their own tongue.

When the buzzing ceased, the lamp hopped its way from Keeper to Keeper back to Bogdan. He set it down more firmly than before. "We do have consciences, Nya, which is why we are speaking to you at all."

"I didn't suggest that you didn't—"

"We have Yaromir," he cut in, making her suck in a breath. "The decision to hold him was not made lightly, nor is our choice to release you without obtaining a promise." He opened his long arms. "The future we hope for is a weaving of many separate threads. You are one, the Windsinger is another.

Holding him would not be just, but it would accomplish our purpose. Releasing him and relying on you is risky, but just. So, many of us would rather take a middle path.

"You may try to take him back, Nya. If you fail, he will remain here to work his healing forever. If you succeed, you must work to overcome the pain that keeps you apart from him. Perhaps your journey in this world will help you do that."

Nya rushed to her feet. "How am I supposed to find him? I—"

"Light will reveal a path to you in the morning."

"A path…?"

But the lamp had gone out.

"Bogdan?" She stared hard at the megaliths, but without the lamp, only darkness looked back at her. The fire in the bowl had been reduced to a few glowing embers. She limped over to it, picked open the klooben's dry skin, and scooped out the warm stuff inside. She ate with a quiet determination, leaving a handful behind for Nenad. Then she curled up by the bowl and tried to sleep.

***

"Wake up, Nya. Wake up, wake up, wake up—"

"I'm awake!" She grimaced as she sat up. Too many cuts. She glared at Nenad's vague form. "It's still dark."

"Yes, and the sky is clear. Do you know how this place will look under a clear sky in daylight? You will wish you were blind. We need to be well on our way down this wretched mountain before that happens."

"I can't. I've been told that the morning light will show me a path, so I have to wait for it. I left you some food. It's by the big bowl." She yawned, listening to his tiny steps on the smooth floor. His lack of surprise over the new items indicated he'd been awake for at least a part of last night's ordeal.

She lay back down and shifted onto her side. As she did, some sort of garment slid off her. She picked it up and explored it with her hands. It was a lightweight hooded cape, probably left by Merima.

The Keeper's name conjured up unpleasant memories. Even so, Nya would be a fool not to accept the cape. She drew it around her and closed her eyes.

"I found the food," Nenad said, "but not the bowl. Ah, and here is a flask."

"No bowl?" She sat up and patted the dim floor. Sure enough, the bowl was gone. The Keepers must have removed it while she slept.

A glance at the megaliths told her the sky was lightening. She could now make out their towering shapes in the gloom. She shook her head at them, wondering at all that had passed only hours before. It seemed like a terrible dream.

Nenad said, "Klooben is not good for my kind. I shall eat it because I'm hungry, but there will consequences."

She touched her belly. "Should I have eaten it? What consequences?"

"You'll be fine. Other peoples have no trouble with klooben."

He had not, she noted, answered her latter question. She set it aside and helped him drink from the flask, which was nearly the length of his body.

After a few gulps, he pushed it aside.

Nya's eyes were closing. She hadn't felt so tired since she downed Nenad's sleeping herbs, but if she dozed off now, she might miss the sign Bogdan had promised her. In the end, she resorted to pain to keep her awake. Lying flat on her back, she let Nenad clean and rewrap her wounds. She found she didn't care anymore what part of her he saw. Pride was a luxury she could no longer afford. The little chima had enough herbal paste left to treat the fresh wounds. The older ones were well scabbed over, or so he said.

When he was done, she thanked him awkwardly, dressed, and stood. "How are we going deal with that mass of crystal on the stairs?"

He shrugged. "Like we deal with everything: as it comes."

"Did you hear what was said last night?"

"Only bits and pieces," he said, but something in his voice and the way he held his mouth made her sure he was lying. Had all the snoring been fake, then? She was about to challenge him on it when he called out, "Step aside, Nya. You are blocking the light."

Her eyes widened. The moment she moved away, a bright fleck of light fell on the top of one of the crystal pillars that ringed the summit. The pillar was straight and pointed.

"Like an arrowhead," Nenad murmured, as if answering her thought. "But what does it point to?" He glanced back at her. "I'm going to find out. Stay here."

"Be careful," she warned as he wove his way through the mess of crystals that lay between the pillars and the dark stone megaliths.

The moment he was gone, she wheeled around and stared at the source of the light. Of course, it came from the gap in one of the standing stones. The sun was rising directly behind it. The beam shot across the stone circle and cut between two other megaliths before hitting the pillar. "For what purpose?" she whispered to herself as she approached it. She ran her hand over the edge of the gap. Its wear spoke of many centuries, perhaps even millennia, since it had been bored. Perhaps the landscape had been different then…

Nenad's high-pitched voice broke through her reverie. "It seems to point to the forbidden bridge."

"Oh?" She turned. "A forbidden bridge to where?"

"I don't know." He gave the klooben skin a sullen kick. "It's forbidden."

"Why? Is it unstable?"

"No."

When he didn't elaborate, Nya said, "What does the bridge span?"

"A bottomless chasm." He kicked the skin again. "The chima are delvers, and they have never found its base."

Nothing, Nya thought, was ever easy in this world. She scooped up the flask and attached it to her belt, then knelt and offered him her shoulder. "Let's go, friend."

"Go…? We can't cross the—"

"We can, and we will. Are you afraid of your path in the Fabric?" Her mouth stiffened with her effort not to smile.

He grunted as he settled in beside her neck. "A forbidden bridge has no place in *any* path."

"Then why did the stone squatters point me in that direction?"

His claws dug into her braids. "Do not call them that!"

"Why? That's what they are. They could've sat with me on the floor, but they chose to look down on me instead, as if I were an insect they enjoyed poking. So stone squatters they are."

Nenad loosed a dramatic sigh but didn't speak again until they were halfway down the mountain. The sun was fully up by then, transforming the eastern side into a blazing torch. Nenad pushed his face into the fabric at her neck to avoid the light. Eyes narrowed to slits, Nya lowered herself down onto a stair and descended carefully on her bottom. When the light behind her eyelids dimmed, she stood again and made her way around the mountain's darker sides. Then down on her bottom again. The cape's deep hood helped block some of the glare, but not enough. She yearned to turn the cape backward so the hood covered her face. Anything to dim the light.

She was creeping along the east side, fingers brushing the wall, when her questing foot slid on loose crystals. She kicked at the debris, then groaned as more tumbled to replace it.

"Wrap your hands again," Nenad mumbled into her neck.

She fumbled with her skirt. "I can't see!" Her eyes were beginning to ache. Even closed, the light seared into them. She nudged the loose crystals aside again and lowered her bottom into the cleared space. Now that she had wedged herself in the mess, she could do nothing save move forward, first nudging and then violently kicking away debris from the steps below her. She reached the other side of the avalanche with fewer injuries than the first time, but so blinded by the light that she wondered if she would ever see again.

It was noon before they came to the path that led away from the stairs. Nya's eyes still ached and blurred, but thankfully she had not been blinded. The colorful snakes made an appearance, reminding her of the crystal's strange properties. Would she ever glimpse it again?

Probably not.

Her steps slowed. Then, despite everything she had been through—or perhaps because of it—she swooped down and filched a shard, slipping it into her belt pouch. Nenad said nothing. He had been unusually silent all day. She recalled his warning about the klooben and hoped he wasn't in discomfort.

As the path crumbled into a weedy patchwork of broken crystal flagstones, she veered off it into the field and wove around dirty chunks of crystal until only weeds and grass remained. She finally stopped at a tall patch of grass. Without a word, Nenad climbed off her, and she dropped to the ground in exhaustion.

The sun was still high when she sat up, her throat dry and her hands quivering with hunger. "Nenad." She found him curled fetal-like around his sack. He lifted his head. His face was pale, and deep furrows cut into his forehead.

"Yes, sweet Nya?"

"We need food and water."

"I know, but we are close to neither. We must either return to the forest or go on to the forbidden bridge. Both are half a day's walk from here."

"Is there food at the bridge?"

"There is a gump pond in some ruins nearby." He winced and gripped his belly. "I shan't move again today."

"I could carry you in my arms."

"No. I cannot bear any movement. Rest with me here, and we'll push on tomorrow."

Nya grazed his back with her finger. She wished she could offer him something to relieve his discomfort. "You're in pain."

"I'll be fine. Why don't you chew some grass? It will take the edge off your hunger." His eyes squeezed shut, and he nestled closer to his sack. She watched him for a time, her teeth worrying her lip. She shouldn't have given him the klooben, but how was she to know it would make him sick?

She plucked some grass and did as he suggested, shifting onto her back to stare at the cloud-streaked sky. The warm day made her drowsy, and she dozed until the sun sank and the ground cooled. She sat up then, fully awake but unable to go anywhere.

The lonely darkness brought to mind the nightmares she had suffered soon after seeing the red Witterkin. Yasna had heard tales of evil becoming a beast. The Witterkin were not evil, but the sort of greed that had overcome her brother *was*. That evil had damaged the Witterkin somehow, creating a new kind of Witterkin that had spread rapidly over the ground. Nya had no doubt that, as the Keepers said, they would have expanded, unchecked, over *this* world. But what about her own—a world full of dangerous weapons and substances? Perhaps it would have ended one way or another—either by the spread of red Witterkin or by the use of poisons needed to destroy them.

She lay back down with a sigh. The stone squatters had laid the fate of both worlds at her feet. It was preposterous.

Absurd. Even if the future depended on the integrity of Yaro's line, he didn't need *her*. Yaro was an attractive man with a good reputation and many long years ahead of him. Someone would fall into his path, a woman prettier and more likeable than Nya.

She swallowed sharply and broke off more grass.

It would have been a nice dream, sweet as frosting, to think that she could be the only one for him. That despite everything, they were meant to be. More: that together they could save two worlds. But the truth was far more mundane. The Keepers had begged Nya to marry him because she had been in the right place at the right time. If Goran's fiancée had dropped into their world instead, they would've demanded the same of her. She let out a sour chuckle. The stone squatters weren't as wise as they thought if they couldn't see humans as people. What made them think Yaro would lie with anyone? He wasn't some stud horse to be led around by the nose.

She had to find him.

Her meeting with the squatters had not changed that goal. It had merely given her a direction. But that was something. That was something indeed.

CHAPTER EIGHT

The next day was soft and warm. Butterflies dipped into the field weeds, and small birds danced in the bright air. Nya would have enjoyed the scene if she weren't hungry and thirsty, reddened by the sun, and cut up like a pincushion. At least her fear of the rhuksies had faded. She hadn't so much as glimpsed one for days.

She walked west around the mountain, her hooded face averted from its brightness. Nenad sat on her shoulder once more, so silent that if it weren't for the weight and warmth of his body, she would have forgotten he was there. A crow dipped down over the grass, black wings flashing blue in the sunlight. As she watched it, a memory surfaced, almost painful in its clarity.

It had been a morning like this, the light soft on the water, wind calm…

Nya wandered the streets of Sundyr while her mother haggled for fine cloth at the market. She paused as she came to a bench near the Windsinger's workshop, her eyes wide. She had sat with Yaro for the first time at a dance only days before, so she was surprised to see him again. She was even more surprised by the dark bird he clasped in his hands.

Yaro was fifteen then, a tall lad who had put on more muscle than others his age. His short dark hair stuck up from his head like porcupine quills. Nya, who was three years younger, stopped in front of him and folded her arms. "It doesn't look happy."

His eyes rose to hers and fell. He stroked the baby crow's fluffy body with a couple of fingers. The action seemed reflexive to her, as if he had done it a hundred times before. "It's dead," he said.

"Oh." Her brow furrowed. "Was it yours – I mean, were you caring for it?"

He shrugged. "I found it on the road a few weeks ago. Brought it home and cleaned it up. It was injured, but I thought it would get better if I fed it. It seemed to…for a while. It even started liking me. Imagine that." He snorted softly. "But this morning it wouldn't eat. I thought it could use some fresh air and sunlight, but by the time I came out here with it, it was dead. Just like that."

"I'm sorry."

He shrugged again and blinked several times. Was he trying not to cry?

She asked, "What will you do?"

"Bury it. What else is there?"

"You could make it a windstone. Isn't that what you and your father do? Give voices to the dead?"

"A stone…" His mouth slackened, and he regarded her with a stunned expression. "I hadn't thought of that. Yes, I could."

"You definitely could."

"I think I will." A smile broke on his face, bright as the sun.

It was the smile that did it. Nya's lips parted, and blood rushed into her cheeks. She looked from his face to his hands and suddenly wanted more than anything to be that bird, stroked by those large, gentle fingers. The strength of her desire confused her. She stood as if pinned to the ground for several moments. Then something loosed her. Muttering a quick goodbye, she took off down the road as if chased by death's hounds.

He did make a stone for the baby crow. It stood in a wind-battered area of Cemetery Hill, croaking its little voice to the sea. Nya had visited it off and on throughout the years.

It was her heart, after all.

***

She rested shortly after noon and sat by Nenad, chewing grass. The mountain was finally behind them, and something shadowy loomed in the distance. Probably the ruins Nenad had spoken of. Her dry mouth watered as she imagined roasting and eating the mudgumps.

A wet hissing sound made her frown and glance at Nenad. "Was that a fart?"

His limp shoulders lifted. "Might have been."

There was another wheezing hiss, followed by a stench like that of rotting fruit. Nya exhaled sharply. "I hope you won't be doing this all day. How am I supposed to carry you on my shoulder while you..." She waved a hand past her nose.

He said, "I warned you there would be consequences. But fear not. It shouldn't last more than a day."

Her eyes widened. "No. I will not carry you through a day of this."

"Alas, I cannot keep up otherwise. I am not well."

"You shouldn't have eaten the klooben."

"I was hungry. And I did not foresee that it would be this bad. Be patient, sweet Nya. It is only a smell."

Smells, Nya thought later, as they approached the ruins, were underestimated. Nenad's flatulence hung like a warm poison cloud around her head. She tried to walk with her face averted, but the terrain made that a challenge. Field grass had given way to shrubs, thickets, and wild vines. The undergrowth was so thick that she resorted to climbing on the heaps of broken stone that were all that remained of what must have been a stately castle gate. An arch loomed over her, swathed in vine yet somehow still standing. Beyond it stood a partial wall with a single curved window. Black soot had scorched the wall around and above the window. The vines had let it be, as if the memory it held was still too painful to be touched.

"What was this place?" she whispered.

"'Twas a grand castle owned by a powerful king. No one knows what happened to him now, but some say he was unkind to his queen and that one day she freed a shapeshifter he kept bound in the dungeon. The shifter changed into a dragon and bore the queen away, and together they united with others against the king. The kingdom fell, and the castle was left to rot. When everyone the shifter knew had died, it returned to this place and has been cursed to guard the forbidden bridge ever since."

Nya, who had been walking across a heap of boulders, paused and risked turning her face to him. "You mean—we will meet this shifter at the bridge?"

"We shall indeed, if the stories are true. The being is known as a greenshifter now, for it has sealed itself to the shape of plants. All who approach it are stopped by a green wall of vines, and if they try to break through that wall… well…" He let out a weak laugh. "You will see what became of them when we get there."

"I thought you said that chima have ventured down into the chasm. They weren't stopped by the green wall?"

"The chasm extends for many hundreds of miles, sweet Nya."

"Then the wall…?

"The wall forms across the bridge's approach to keep people from crossing it."

"Maybe humans will be allowed to pass," she ventured weakly.

"That is possible. Ah, the mudgump pool is close now. Do you see that broken statue? It is there."

The shallow pond had probably been beautiful in its day. Perhaps it had stood at the center of a stately garden. All that remained of it now was a foot or two of sludge, fed by a thin trickle of water that emerged from the rubble. Nya removed her cape and boots before plunging into the muck after the sucking mudgumps. She soon found she didn't have the strength she'd had in the forest. Still, she managed to pull out two and with Nenad's help drained them before returning to the weedy bank. They built a small fire using charred bits of wood pulled from the rubble and ate the gumps while they were still hot, Nenad more tentatively than Nya. Energized by the food, she gathered nine more and trussed together what she did not eat. It took time and patience to fill the flask from the trickling stream, but it was well worth the trouble. Her knowledgeable guide would be useless once they crossed the bridge into unfamiliar terrain. The prospect brought back the sense of helplessness she had experienced on her first day in this place. At least now she had some guidance from the stone squatters.

She let Nenad sleep for a while. Her own eyes felt glued open.

Bogdan had warned that if she failed to bring Yaro home, he would remain here to work his healing forever. What did "work his healing" mean? Was Yaro trapped somewhere against his will, cursed by some enchantment to play day and night while aware of his surroundings? It was hard to imagine a worse fate. Even if she found him, such an experience would ruin windsinging for him forever after. Of course, this would not have occurred to Bogdan, who seemed unaware that humans were people like himself.

She rose with a sigh and woke Nenad. "How far is the bridge?" she asked as he settled on her shoulder.

"Not more than a half-hour's walk from here."

"Good." She walked along the bank, following the brightness of the late afternoon sun, the flask swinging from her left wrist.

"Nya, I think you were right about humans being allowed to pass. Why else would the Keepers have pointed you here?"

"Exactly."

"But where does that leave *me*?"

"I'll have to hide you." She frowned. The only place where he could remain fully concealed was under her clothing. But that meant…

She suppressed a groan. "You'll have to lie under my frock and cling to my belly."

"But that would make you look…"

"Pregnant. I know." She edged around a collapsed wall and threaded her way through a debris-filled passageway. "You will have to keep absolutely still."

"I can do that."

"Then do it now. I don't want the shifter to see or hear you before we reach the bridge." She paused at the other side of the passageway, batting back a cobweb of weeds and vine as she opened the strings of her cape.

"What about my conception pillow?"

Nya cringed at the thought of that stained sack against her skin, but he didn't sound eager to part with it. "Take it with you," she said.

Nenad lowered himself down her chest and under the front of her frock. His claws brushed her bare skin, and she winced as he pressed on the wounds left by the rhuksie. He shifted awkwardly, straining the fabric, until he finally settled, his little body stretching horizontally across her middle with the sack just above him. "You're too high," she warned.

"I can't go any lower. Your belt..."

She loosened her belt and let it drop a couple of inches so that it sat on her hips. "Now?"

He wriggled lower and went still. She tugged out some extra fabric, then ran a hand lightly over his back. "I think it will do. The sack rounds it out a bit, and the cape hides most of it anyway." She retied the strings.

He mumbled something against her skin. When she asked him to repeat it, he lifted his tiny head and said, "The greenshifter is dangerous."

"He didn't seem bad in the story—"

"That tale was not recorded by chima, so it cannot be trusted. In truth, no one knows who the shifter is or why it guards the bridge. If the green wall forms, do not attempt to push through it."

"Understood," she said gruffly and stepped out of the passageway.

The walk to the bridge was uncomfortable. It was the hottest part of the day, and even when the ruins shaded her, she felt suffocated by the humidity. She began to regret hiding Nenad so early. He was like a slick hot water bottle, sliding around in her own sweat, even with his claws fastened to her belt. She was about to ask if he had been wrong about the half hour when she glimpsed an odd length of cloud in the distance. She slowed and squinted. "Not mountains," she breathed. The shape was too low and far too near. The more she observed it, the more certain she became that it was fog.

She trudged on and a few minutes later spied the chasm with the hanging bridge cutting across it. The fog hovered like a gate on the opposite side, concealing what lay beyond. Nya stumbled through some thick ferns to an old path that led to the chasm. She halted at a low stone wall that lined the chasm's edge and peered around. The chasm did appear bottomless, even more so than the crack she'd tumbled down after her encounter with the rhuksie. As for the bridge, it was so wreathed in vine that she couldn't make out a single board or length of rope. But vines were sturdy, she told herself. If the bridge broke, she could always climb them back to the top.

The thought chilled her.

She scanned the wall, flicking back a dark braid that had come loose from where it had been bound at the top of her head. No one was here, and there was no evidence of recent habitation. Perhaps the shifter had finally found peace. Should she remove Nenad?

Better that he stayed put. If she came upon a missing board, she might trip, but Nenad would fall right through it. She nudged a vine with her foot, trying to discover how the bridge was secured to the cliff. An odd rustling made her look up.

She stumbled back, her eyes wide in horror.

The vines on the bridge were coming off at an incredible speed, each one as alive and powerful as a limb. In mere seconds, they had massed together to form a thick, man-shaped body with a hunched back and cowled head. The shifter stood in front of the bridge, the vines at his chest rasping as he drew breath. At twenty feet high, he towered over her.

Nya turned to run, but a powerful voice thundered at her, rooting her to the spot.

"Stop!"

Swaying a little, she turned and met the creature's hollow black eyes. Beyond him, the bridge, bare now of vine, was revealed to be littered with polished bones.

The shifter tilted its massive head. "You wished to cross."

She swallowed and tried to push out a sound. "Yes."

"Why?"

Several moments passed while she gathered her thoughts. "I'm trying to find my friend and return him to the human world. The Keepers on Crystal Mountain pointed me here, or I would never have found this place."

"How did they point you here?"

"By means of light shining through a gap in a standing stone." Her shoulders tensed. The explanation sounded preposterous, even when compared to a man made of vine.

The shifter's shadowy face betrayed no expression. As Nya searched for something else to say, something cool touched her leg. She looked down and squeaked. A vine was snaking up her leg.

"Be still," the shifter growled.

Nya responded with a whimper. Nenad was trembling now, his claws pinching into her as if he wanted to sink into her skin. The vine slid over her cape, pausing at her middle before hurrying to her head. Leaves tickled her neck and ear, grazed a cheekbone, an eyebrow. Nya shivered. She thought she could sense the force that enlivened the vine, a buzz of power that made her stomach clench.

At last, it dropped and returned to the shifter. "Remove your boots."

Boots. "All right." She tried to kick them off, but sweat had glued them to her feet. Carefully, she bent down to remove them. As her thigh bumped Nenad's back, a sound like that of a duck being stepped on pierced the air. She froze, blood roaring in her ears. She said weakly, "I'm sorry. I ate something that disagreed with me."

The shifter made no reply.

Her boots removed, Nya waited while the vine explored her feet and ankles. Something wet dribbled down her leg. She mashed her frock against it, catching Nenad's urine before it found her feet. At last, the vine withdrew, and she was ordered to put her boots back on. Her thoughts reeled as she obeyed him. *All those bone shards on the bridge…* What would she do if he attacked her or Nenad? It would be quick. She had seen how fast the vines could move. If she hadn't lost Yasna's blade to the lioness, she might have stood a chance. Without it, she was at his mercy.

She straightened and then flinched. The creature had edged closer while she was replacing her boots. He was only a few feet from her now, the black holes of his eyes boring into hers.

His voice grazed her—a whisper of rustling leaves, forming words somehow. "You and the chima may cross the bridge." He paused when Nenad made a little squeak and went on more ponderously, "But neither of you may return. Consider that well before leaving." He stepped aside and was still.

Nya blinked. She looked from him to the littered bridge, then back again. It must be a trap. He wouldn't have released them so easily.

She shifted from foot to foot. Clearing her throat, she said, "Why are you letting us go?"

"That is not your concern."

She took a tentative step. "What lies beyond the fog?"

Silence. She repeated the question, but he wouldn't answer.

Time to go. If indeed she *could* go.

She strode to the bridge on stiff legs and grasped hold of the guide ropes. It had to be at least fifty feet long. The wooden slats looked bright and solid, as if they had been newly placed. The structure shifted under her weight but did not creak or sag. Her boots tapped irregularly as she stepped over and around the bones. When she had put the last of them behind her, she fixed her gaze ahead and walked on with a steady step until she reached the opposite side. The moment her foot touched land, vines rustled behind her. She wheeled around to find the shifter gone and the bridge wreathed in vine once again. The ruined castle grounds stood beyond, looking ominous in the falling light.

There'd be no going back now. Chest tight, she walked into the fog.

CHAPTER NINE

The fog dissipated after perhaps a dozen yards, and Nya paused to stare at the landscape before her. She stood at the mouth of a lush pass. Green hills swept up on either side like ocean waves. A stream flowed between them, its banks overhung by clumps of reeds.

Now what? she thought. How long would this wretched journey take? She hadn't known what to expect when she stepped through the fog, but it wasn't this pastoral scene. Yaro's windsinging continued, unchanged from before. She undid her cape strings, drew the damp chima out of her frock, and held him up. He sucked in a startled breath at the view.

She asked, "Have you heard anything about this place?"

"No." His head tilted up. "Something strange about the hills."

Her nose wrinkled at the stench of sweat and urine wafting off him. "You and I are going to wash."

She endured the smells until she reached the winding stream, then she removed him from her shoulder, shed her clothes to her undergarments and pushed through the reeds to the crystal water. Bathing her cut-up body was a tentative, painful ordeal and she did not rush it. Afterward, she scrubbed her frock until only the deepest stains remained. She wrung it as best she could before draping it over cattails. Nenad, free now of foul odors, was in better spirits as they sat near the bank and ate what remained of the mudgumps.

The evening transitioned into a warm night. With no fuel for a fire, they lay down in the grass near the stream and tried to sleep. Nya had tossed and turned for some minutes before sitting up and touching Nenad's arm. "Did you hear the greenshifter say we couldn't go back?"

"Yes."

"I never asked if you were all right with that."

"If I wasn't, I would have said something."

The stiffness in her shoulders eased. "That's what I thought, but I wanted to be sure." She lay back and stared up at the hazy night sky. When Nenad's wheezy snoring didn't resume, she said sleepily, "Did you sense something from the vines, like a buzz of power?"

"No. Did you?"

She had. An echo of it still moved through her, like a strange voice in a dark room. What did that mean? She wanted to discuss it with Nenad, but an uneasy note in his voice made her edge away from the subject. "I thought I did, but it was probably just my imagination. Sleep well."

She woke at dawn, hungry again and eager to move on. With no other water source in sight, it made sense to follow the river, at least for a while. While Nenad slept, she dressed in her now dry clothes, then pulled up several cattails, rinsed the edible roots, and peeled them with her teeth to remove the excess fiber. Her grandmother's plant book had suggested boiling, but without a fire, she had to settle on eating them raw. She left one for Nenad, but when he woke, he refused it, saying he had learned his lesson about plants he shouldn't eat.

Nya walked, and rested, and then walked again, her hood down and cape unfastened. The only creature she spied was the occasional grasshopper. She might have enjoyed the quiet, peaceful place if it weren't for her building unease. Nenad must have felt it too, for his cheerful singing ceased, and he nestled against her neck. A mist gathered on the hills, and as the afternoon bled into another evening, the sky changed from blue to shades of rose and purple. The pass began to feel enclosed, like a four-poster bed wrapped in colored silks.

Something moved in her peripheral vision. She slowed and eyed the hill on the left. The mist on it had thinned, and as she looked on, the pale outcrop that capped the hill smoothed and shifted. Nya stiffened, and her wide, unbelieving eyes fixed on the outcrop. Limbs were taking shape from the rocks, the muscled curve of a leg, a bare buttock, two arms, one twisted the wrong way. No. It was not wrong. As the last of the mist shredded away, a second body came into view—a supple female one, lying beneath the first.

A deep sigh shook the air, and the bodies slammed together. Nya's face heated, and she turned aside—only to be assaulted by a second pair on the opposite hill. The lovers were huge, at least one hundred yards long, and as their thrusting intensified, the ground shook and trembled. Nya trudged on, her mouth a thin line, her fingers tightly clenched. She tried not to stare at either one of the couples, but as their breathing grew heavier, she could not look away. Her steps slowed, her lips parted, and a flush of heat moved through her.

Suddenly one cried out—a sound every bit as loud as thunder. Nya tripped and fell. Despite the soft grass, she managed to skin her elbow. She felt around for Nenad and found him crouched by some reeds. "Are you hurt?" Her voice sounded raw in her ears.

He scrambled back onto her shoulder. "No. But thanks for asking." He said something more, but the thunder of another groan swallowed it up. This time, Nya fixed her eyes on the ground ahead as she walked. Bodies writhed and tangled in her peripheral vision. The air smelled of sweat and musk. After a while, the pounding ceased and the air became filled with soft whispers. It was a warm, intimate space.

Nya's chest ached. Despite her resolution to ignore the giants, she could not stop herself from feeling an echo of their passion. She halted finally and ogled a glistening pair. She had not glimpsed a face before, but now it was as though her direct stare revealed it: the shadowy eyes and curving lips that bumped his lover's skin in soft kisses. Nya ran a hand down her arm, wishing she could experience such closeness.

"Nya?"

She cleared her throat. "It's nothing. I'm just tired."

She walked on, but it was twilight before she had put the giants behind her. After letting Nenad down, she gathered more reeds, stripped the roots, and ate them without pleasure. "I wish I had something for you," she said. Nenad assured her he was fine and told her not to worry.

Nya settled in the grass across from him, her head in her hands. A deep loneliness welled up in her, mingled with a helplessness she neither understood nor wanted to explore. She peered at Nenad's dim form. "Have you ever wanted to be someone else?"

"Do you mean…?"

"Not a chima."

"To be honest, no. I've always desired to wander the world and couldn't have done so with children dogging my heels."

"That's fair. But what if the chima weren't respected like they are now? What if no one wanted their stories and maps and didn't care if they ever came back?" She could feel the weight of his eyes on her.

After a long pause, he said, "That would be a great tragedy."

"Yes."

"Why do you ask me this question?"

She shrugged, then realized he couldn't see her gesture in the darkness. "Because not everyone has a fair shake at life, Nenad. You're fortunate to be respected, but it could've gone the other way, and then you might have wished you weren't born a chima."

She waited for him to either agree or disagree. Instead, he said, "It sounds as if you speak from experience."

And that, she thought later, was all the prodding she had needed to talk about her own injustices—the old herbal that had led people to believe she was a witch, the whispering and warding signs done in her presence, the fear she invoked in children. Talking things out had always made her feel better, and she had believed this would be no different, but long before she'd finished, her own words had begun to disgust her. Hadn't some of her actions contributed to her bad reputation? And how terrible had her life been anyway? She had been well-off, with enough independence to choose her pastimes and a kind friend in Yasna. And she'd still had a smattering of clients who'd braved her reputation to come to her door. It hadn't been a bad life. She certainly couldn't compare it to the hypothetical rejection of the chima.

She sighed and glanced at Nenad's sleeping form. Thankfully, he had drifted off before she'd finished telling her story. Hunger and his recent illness were likely taking a greater toll on him than he'd let on. She could only hope they came upon a mudgump pond or some other food source tomorrow.

She shifted onto her back and tried to sleep. But in the quiet darkness, her loneliness returned. The giants tangled behind her closed eyes, reminding her of her own lack of romantic intimacy. It wasn't something that had concerned her before, but now it was there, like a seed, planted and spreading roots.

She could never unsee the giants' lovemaking; it would haunt her forever. The Keepers must have known that. Why else would they have set her on this painful path?

Nenad was awake before her the next morning, gnawing on some sort of hard berry. "I fell asleep before your tale was told," he said. "I apologize for that."

"It wasn't worth telling anyway." She groaned as she got to her feet. Every time she thought she was better, her injuries disagreed.

"Your bandages need changing."

"I know. I'll see what I can do."

"I could—"

"No. Today you need to conserve energy." She turned before he could argue and dragged up a dozen cattails. After the meal, she was so sick that she could neither change her bandages nor walk. Nenad clucked his tongue at her while he tended to the worst of her injuries. The sun was fully up by then. A soft wind blew over the grasses, creating green waves. Clutching her sore belly, Nya stood and squinted at the landscape ahead of them. The hills grew flatter, and some pale structures poked out of the earth.

"What is it?" Nenad queried.

"I'm not sure. Hold on, I'll show you." She picked him up and hoisted him over her head with both hands. After a few moments, he went as still as death. "What do you see?" she prodded, peering up at his tiny face.

In response, his hand went to his mouth and a sound, somewhere between a sob and a cry, choked out of him.

"Nenad—?"

"'Tis the lady! Oh, blessed day!" Tears flowed down his face. Nya lowered her arms but he pleaded for her to keep him elevated so he could continue watching the Lake Mother.

"I can do better than that," Nya said, setting him on her shoulder. "Let's go to her."

He stood on her shoulder, clutching her braids as she walked, growing more restless the closer they came to the Lake Mother.

And as the full scene revealed itself, even Nya caught her breath. A white lake glistened in the sunlight. The giantess lay on her back in it, the top of her face, her breasts, the huge bump of her pregnant belly, and her toes peeking from the liquid. Her eyes were closed, and her expression was one of serenity and contentment. Milk seeped in a constant stream from her pale breasts, creating slow ripples that lapped against the shore. "She's beautiful," Nya said, feeling some strong emotion stir in her.

Nenad was speechless. No songs of praise bubbled from his lips. Perhaps he didn't trust them to be good enough for his lady. Nya could have pointed out that this giantess was not human and therefore could not create a lake of human milk, but she kept her lips sealed. As she neared the shore, Nenad scrambled down her, forcing her to halt, and rushed to the lapping shore. He knelt on one knee, closed his eyes, and murmured a prayer. Then he secured his sack around his waist and waded in.

"Don't disturb her!" Nya hissed, but he didn't pause. When the lake grew too deep, he swam, his small body bobbing in the ripples as he approached a breast. The giantess' eyelids didn't twitch as he began to climb one. She was either too deeply asleep or so massive that she couldn't sense Nenad's slight weight. Wisely, he chose the drier side and after perhaps half an hour of struggling crested the peak of the mountain-like breast. Such a sight. Nya shook her head. She sat cross-legged on the shore, her fingers grazing a bit of milk when it lapped close to her.

Nenad stood awkwardly by the nipple and stretched out his hands. Soon he was so drenched in milk that Nya could no longer see him. A line from his poem came to her mind. *Ah, the sweet teats of the Lake Mother.*

It *was* sweet. After her first taste, she brought it to her mouth in handfuls until milk dribbled down her chin to her own breasts. What would it be like to produce such a nourishing liquid?

Merima's mocking words rang in her ears. *You know nothing of your own mortal magics.*

So the Keepers had shoved them in her face. Here. Look at everything you choose not to have. Look at this, and this.

She drew back, wiping an arm across her mouth.

The day passed slowly into night. Nya fell asleep listening to the lady's soft breathing and the gurgling of her milk. She woke at dawn to find Nenad standing beside her, cheeks flushed again with health. A wistful smile hung on his face.

"Nya, I cannot leave her. You must go on alone."

She sat up, fully awake now. "But you promised you'd help me find Yaro."

He shook his head. "I never made such a promise. *You* swore to find the lake of milk *after* you found Yaro. I said I would help, but that help depended on the sequence of events you outlined."

"You sound like my family lawyer."

Nenad ignored the comment and laid his small hand on her arm. "I know you will find him. You don't need me anymore."

Nya's heart had begun to hammer. Though she hated to admit it, she had come to rely on Nenad's confident presence; even his steady weight on her shoulder had begun to feel like a warm hand. She searched for a way to dissuade him. "This is a bad idea. You can't stay here anyway. One of these days the lady will give birth, and her child will probably empty this lake. What will you do then?"

"Perhaps I'll move on and explore this part of the world. Now that I'm here, I can do whatever I wish, go wherever I fancy. Thanks to you, sweet Nya." He bowed deeply and strode away.

She watched him with wide eyes. "I'll miss you," she said.

"And I you," he said over his shoulder. "If you ever have a child, name him Nenad. That was not meant to be a joke," he added as she let out a soft snort. He waded into the lake and swam toward a breast.

She would probably never see him again.

There was nothing to stay for, but it felt strange to walk away alone, so she lingered for a time, filling the flask with milk, examining her injuries and removing cloth as needed. But eventually she had no reason to loiter. She waved to

Nenad, who was sprawled across the bridge of the lady's nose, but he didn't seem to see her.

Alone again. A light breeze tickled the grass. She wondered if the wind river ever flowed this way. So far, she had seen no evidence of it. She hiked back to the stream and followed it, glancing back every so often at the lake.

Until it was gone, swallowed up by a grassy rise. Her hand swept over her empty shoulder and neck, the place where Nenad had clung to her braids through countless hours of walking. *There, and then gone forever.*

The day passed slowly. She rested once and then forced herself on. As the afternoon veered toward evening, the almost flattened hills swept up again, and this time they were of solid stone. The land between them narrowed to some point in the distance. Nya couldn't tell if the hills actually met or if some sort of canyon slid through them. She walked into a twilight made deeper by shadows cast by the stone hills. When it was nearly dark, a point of light bloomed ahead of her. By then, the stream had shrunk to a fist-sized trickle. Nya trod on the rocks where water had once ran, her footsteps echoing off the smooth stone walls.

She slowed and stared at the warm light. And that was when she heard it: the faint but unmistakable sound of deep panting. It reminded her of the labored breathing women made in childbirth. But though faint, the sound was too vast to come from a human woman. Perhaps a giantess? Warmth brushed her face; it seemed to emanate from the enticing light ahead. Driven by some unfathomable urge, she hurried toward it, her head lowered against the brightness.

A long, heavy breath roared out, and the light widened. Both came from the gap ahead of her, as if the stone walls were legs and the gap a sighing birth canal. Nya lifted her head to it, her eyes burning from the light and maybe from unshed tears. A new life was coming. She could almost sense it. Smell it in the heat radiating from the widening hole. Her heart pressed painfully against her chest. *Go back*, her mind said, *you don't know what this is. It feels like the birth of a star.* But she could not. She would walk into the light until it blazed on her. She removed her cape and clutched it with one hand.

Another labored breath, and then a roar like fire. The light flared, blinding her. She did not remember falling over. She knew only warmth and a pain in her core that threatened to tear her open.

And then she knew no more.

CHAPTER TEN

"I want to make you a windstone," Yaro said.

Nya stood on Bell Hall's back patio, her face trained on the dark sea. She didn't know why she had come here, scarcely a year after her mother's death. At the funeral, she had made it clear to Yaro that while she didn't hold the accident against him, she no longer felt comfortable in his presence. And yet here she was. Perhaps she needed closure.

She wouldn't consider the other possibility -- that she had come just to see *him.*

"It's early for that," she said, her voice as tight as her crossed arms. "I'm not dead yet and don't expect to be for some time."

He shifted closer, and it took all her self-control not to bolt. He had grown since she'd last seen him, both in height and breadth. But his deep, almost musical voice was just the same as it had been.

While these observations interested her, any pleasure she might have taken from them was ruined by a creeping sense of dread, one that made her stiffen and her belly clench. She couldn't control the reaction. Her mother's death still felt fresh, and being in Yaro's presence made it feel horribly close and real.

Why was she here?

"I know," he replied. "But my ideas have broadened since you said I could make one for a crow." He sighed, leaning back. "When was that, three years ago now?"

"At least."

Why were they talking about this? He hadn't seen her in a year, and all he could think about was windstone. "Yaro – "

"I want to make a stone for your life,*" he said, turning so that he faced her full on, "not your death. I'll place it in a sea cave, where the wind will blow it all day. And no one will know it's there but you and me."*

Her throat had gone dry. "Why?"

"I don't know. Maybe I'm superstitious."

"That's not an answer."

He shrugged and cleared his throat. "Maybe the stronger a voice you have in this world, the longer you'll live."

Nya's brows rose. Had her mother's unexpected death made him fearful for Nya's life?

No. The truth rushed on her suddenly, making her gasp. This wasn't for her – it was for him. It was a grave marker for the girl she'd once been, the girl who had sat with him at dances and during his lunch breaks. He wanted to listen to that girl's voice again, even when she was no longer there.

Tears pricked her eyes. She wheeled away, felt him grasp her hand, and shook it off. "No! You have to let me go, Yaro. We were never truly together anyway, so there's nothing to miss."

"Then why are you crying?" His voice was rough.

She shook her head, swallowing hard. There were no words left for either of them. She turned and ran, leaving him alone on the patio, framed by the black sea.

***

Nya blinked at the black stone wall she lay alongside, remembering the exchange. Her fingers opened, and she stared at them thoughtlessly. Then it was as if she woke from a long dream.

Her heartbeat quickened, and she sat up on an elbow. What had happened? She had been walking into a blazing hole, because… Because she had known somehow that a new life was coming and she'd wanted to be near it? She pushed a hand against her eyes. That didn't make sense. Yet it must have happened, for the sense of wonder it had given her was with her still. And her cape was gone. She must have dropped it when she fell.

She set the matter aside and strove to order her thoughts. Where was she now, and how had she gotten here?

She got to her feet against the wall, only to buckle and almost collapse. Her head spun from the effort of standing. She leaned her forehead on the wall and drew in long, steadying breaths. When had she last eaten a real meal? The days blurred together, like a muddy palette. She had gorged on mudgumps at the castle ruins two days ago, and before that, klooben at Crystal Mountain. On a good day in this world, she'd managed a single proper-sized meal. She might have endured this reduced diet with ease if she'd spent her days lounging in a comfortable chair, but since she'd arrived here, she had been extremely active—trudging up hills, mountains, and stairs, and acquiring injuries as she went. Now, it was all catching up with her. She sensed the wrongness in her body, a deep lethargy and disinterest to do anything more taxing than lean against a mysterious stone wall. She removed the flask of milk and took a couple of gulps before reluctantly replacing the cap. She didn't know when she'd find food again.

Turn around, keep moving.

She steadied herself and turned.

A startling sight met her eyes.

She stood against the curving wall of a chamber the size of Crystal Mountain's entire summit. The floor was of solid, polished crystal, but unlike the smooth floor at the center of the standing stones, this one radiated a deep, lambent light. In fact, it seemed to be the only light source in the round chamber. Crystal pillars at least four feet in diameter stood along the wall, their tops reaching up into a ceiling so high, they vanished in shadow. A telltale curling of light deep within them identified their source as Crystal Mountain. Another, smaller ring of pillars stood several yards closer to the room's center, this one made of wood so blackened with age that if not for the texture, she would have taken it for stone. The wooden pillars were perhaps two feet in diameter and stood at a height of about twenty feet. Their surfaces were engraved with strange designs in a style reminiscent of the diagrams in her grandmother's herbal.

She shoved aside the implications of that thought and examined the room more closely. Both the color and layout of the inner and outer circles reminded her of Crystal Mountain's stone rings. If the chamber was meant to mimic the mountain's summit, then perhaps she would find a door out, and even stairs leading down. She hoped she wouldn't have to face another long descent.

How had she gotten here? a persistent inner voice asked. Was this what lay beyond the blazing hole?

Focus. She needed to find a door. She edged along the wall behind a crystal pillar, her soft steps and Yaro's playing the only sounds in her ears. It amazed her that the windsong reached inside such an enclosed space. Was it louder now, or did she imagine it?

She was trying to recall how it had sounded in the Witterwylds, when movement in her peripheral vision made her pull up short. She threw a sharp glance toward the center of the room.

Nothing. Or at least, nothing now. She began walking again, and the movement promptly resumed. After stopping and starting several more times, she became certain of its source: the wooden pillars. Somehow, they were turning, like spokes in a great wheel. But the movement was only discernible in her peripheral vision. Was she seeing it at all?

She had paused once more to stare at the pillars when a narrow gleam of light caught her attention. It emanated from one of the wooden pillars facing the inside of the circle. Another pillar must have blocked her sight of it earlier.

As she focused on the pillar, her eyes widened. She had been wrong. The light wasn't coming from the pillar at all, but from a figure standing against the pillar. The brightness emanated from his chest, and it pulsed with the rise and fall of the windsinging.

Nya's breath stilled, half drawn in her throat. Though he was at least fifty feet away, she knew him. She would know him at a hundred feet. At two hundred. Her mouth opened, and she tried to push out a sound, but nothing came. Her fists clenched. She swallowed convulsively, then drew in a sharp breath and screamed. Yaro's name ripped out of her, echoing off the fantastically high walls. It felt like a kind of release.

She was breathing hard as the echo faded, her pleading eyes fixed on Yaro. He hadn't moved. Why not? Any man would have jolted at that cry. What was wrong? What had happened to him?

She shoved away from the wall and raced toward him, heart pounding in her throat. But she had underestimated the slickness of the floor. Her bad ankle unbalanced her, and she slipped and fell, knees slamming onto the hard crystal.

She moaned and tried to get up. Blood seeped through the fabric of her skirt. Her old wounds from Crystal Mountain must have broken open. As she struggled to stand, blood wetted the gleaming floor, making it even more slippery. She glanced up at Yaro. He still hadn't moved.

When she finally got to her feet again, another wave of dizziness almost dropped her. She dragged in several steadying breaths before starting forward again, walking as if on ice. Fifty feet had never felt so far. She had grown too weak. What would she do once she had him? Bogdan hadn't told her how she and Yaro might leave this world.

At last, she reached the wooden pillars. As she stepped between them, a strange pressure in the air squeezed her, making her gasp and step quickly through. The pressure eased, and she paused, lifting her head from the treacherous floor. Yaro was only a few yards away now—close enough for her to make him out clearly.

He did not seem conscious. His eyes were half-lidded and his mouth hung open, twitching. Yet he was not at rest either. His muscles were corded, his fists clenched as if he fought something in a waking dream. Or endured great pain. She counted several red welts on his neck and face. His windsinging had indeed gotten louder and seemed to emanate from the terrible brightness in his core.

A whimper clawed out of her. She crossed the space to him and seized his wrists. He didn't respond to the touch; his arms remained tense and flat to the pillar. She tugged him toward her, using her weight as leverage. Still, he didn't budge. What was holding him? No ropes or chains bound him to the pillar. "Yaro!"

In a fit of frustration, she kicked and slapped him, all the while screaming his name, but he didn't budge an inch. It was as if his own music were a spell—or curse, as Nenad might say—holding him fast to the pillar.

At last, she collapsed on the floor, trembling from the effort. A terrible despair welled up in her; tears clouded her vision. *You can* try *to take him back,* Bogdan had said. There was little hope in that statement. Perhaps he had not expected her to succeed. He and the other Keepers might even have created this space. She had no clue as to the extent of their power or what they considered to be "just." They had given her a chance to retrieve him, and that was all. If she failed, they would continue to use him as they saw fit.

And she *was* failing. She leaned her elbows on her knees and rubbed her temples. *Think.* Yaro had been locked into some sort of semiconscious state, like a sleepwalker. If she could knock him fully out, his windsinging might falter, and he might come away from the pillar. But how would she manage that? Hit him over the head with the flask?

She jerked upright. The yellow-leafed plant! Her hand flew to her belt pouch, and she fumbled through its contents. At last, she recognized the familiar shape of the plant's leaf. She dragged herself to her feet and held it up between her thumb and forefinger. Half a leaf should do, but he would not swallow it as it was—*if* he could swallow at all. She chewed the leaf to a mash and then, holding his mouth open with one hand, pushed the sticky mess of leaf and saliva to the back of his throat. She followed it up with a trickle of milk from the flask. "Swallow," she begged. "Please." She tilted his head back against the stone and massaged his throat. Milk dribbled from his lips.

Finally, he swallowed.

Nya fell back with a cry. She had done it. Or at least half of it. She lay down at his feet and waited.

Her heavy eyes wanted to close. She must have swallowed some of the leaf juice. Unable to fight the drug, she fell into a restless sleep. Dreams came on her like inky webs, full of creaking wood and whispering voices. In every dream, she struggled to waken, only to be drawn back down into sleep again.

When she finally sat up, Yaro was gone, and Bogdan stood in his place at the pillar. His face was like a storm cloud, and his black eyes bore into hers. "You must not forget your purpose," he said, biting off each word as if they weighed too much for his mouth. "If you do, you will regret it."

"Where's Yaro?" She wheeled around, searching the chamber's empty space, then came awake with a sharp intake of breath.

Truly awake this time.

The first thing she noticed was the silence. The light in Yaro's core was almost out, and with it, his windsinging. Abruptly, one of his knees buckled. Worried he would hurt himself falling to the floor, she scrambled to her feet and gripped his slackening body. She had forgotten how large he was. How heavy. What would she do if he collapsed on her?

The light in his core went dark.

A pressure in her ears, a terrible ringing. She pushed her head into his shoulder, wanting to run from it, wanting to scream. Yaro collapsed then, and she fell.

PART THREE:

SEEING THROUGH CRYSTAL

CHAPTER ELEVEN

Nya woke slowly, her mind fuzzy and her body warm. She wanted to return to oblivion, but her stomach ached and her mouth felt sticky. Her eyes cracked open. She was in her own room, lying on her own bed. How had she gotten here? And where was Yaro?

A chair creaked, and Yasna was at her side. "You're awake!" She flung open the chamber door and shouted for food and water.

Nya swallowed and rasped out a word. "Yaro?"

Yasna swept back to her side and brushed Nya's forehead. The gesture seemed thoughtless, reflexive. It made Nya wonder how long Yasna had been caring for her this way. "He's fine, Nitty. He spent the night here, looking in on you. But after the doctor came and said you just needed sleep, he left." Her mouth twitched, and she regarded Nya with a wary but intense interest.

Nya grinned at her helplessly. Yaro lived. She didn't know if the Keepers had been forced to release him or if

Nya's own actions had prompted a release. But did it matter? He was back, and Bogdan be damned. She wanted to jump up and hug Yasna, but just sitting up made her aware of all the injuries she had brought with her from the other world. She glanced at the distant mountains outside her window. The sky was iron gray, and as she stared at it, lightning flickered.

The door opened, and Yasna retrieved a platter from the servant.

She spoke while Nya ate, her long nails tapping lightly on the wooden chair arms.

"I came by yesterday morning. Was worried about you after what you said about your brother and his friends. The stableman said you'd gone out with Yaromir not an hour before, so I turned my horse up the path and followed the tracks to the cave." She leaned back, drawing a noisy breath through stiff lips. "I thought you were done for. I couldn't budge you, not you or Yaromir, so I galloped back here and rounded up all the servants I could find. Two of them wouldn't go up that horrid path through the Witterkin, even to save your life. But the stableman was enough, him being a big man and all. I was so afraid you wouldn't make it, but you both came through alive, the gods be praised."

She paused. Nya had stopped eating. Her hand lay open on the tray, and warm butter trickled down the toast to her fingers. At last she spluttered, "I've only been unconscious for a day?"

The wariness returned to Yasna's face. "You were pulled out yesterday afternoon." She cleared her throat and leaned back, as if she couldn't stand the weight of Nya's eyes. "I washed and dressed you. Saw to your wounds myself, though the nosy servants kept wanting in, and Faina came by, desperate to speak to you. I had the maid kindly shoo her away."

"Thank you," Nya said, her throat tightening. "For everything."

Yasna made no reply. She looked old and tired as she got up and crossed to the window. Raindrops tapped against the pane, and there was another flash of lightning, followed swiftly by thunder. Her voice slid out of it, calm but brittle. "I've never seen a body so cut-up and dirty. You looked like something my cat chewed and spat out. Your frock isn't fit for rags, and your boots have walked themselves to hell and back. While I tried to untangle your hair, I found everything from sticks and leaves to tiny bits of—well, I don't right know what to call them, but they looked an awful lot like shed animal claws. Yaromir had a few welts, but nothing like…" She shook her head and rubbed her eyes. "Some of your injuries were well scabbed over, Nitty. They must have been days old. And well tended to."

Nya wiped her fingers on the cloth by the tray and took a swallow of tea. "I got them while I was in the Witterkin."

Yasna turned from the window to face her. "How?"

"You know how." She spread some jam on the bread. "There's only one way I could have come out looking like that in such a short time. You just won't admit it." After a pause, she went on eating. Her appetite was fierce, but she tried to take small bites and chew slowly.

The floor creaked as Yasna paced. "Maybe you're right. But the court won't believe fairy stories, and it's the court you'll have to convince. See, the stableman went to town this morning to report what he saw, and—"

"What *did* he see? In the cave, I mean."

"Three stinking corpses, almost covered by Witterkin—"

"Green Witterkin?"

"Yes. All of them green. Yaromir's head and shoulders were in them too, and you were beside him with your arms in the Witterkin."

"And Yaro's...bellows?"

"That and the windstone are still sitting by the cave wall. Yaromir said it was too dangerous to retrieve them, and I'm inclined to agree."

Nya took another cautious bite. "You said something about court. Am I being accused of something?"

Yasna's jaw tightened, and she resumed her pacing. "You're in bad shape, Nitty. The stableman didn't see the worst of your injuries, but I did, and I know what the court doctor will think if he's made to examine you—that you were roughed up by your brother's friends to keep quiet. So." She stopped and looked pointedly at Nya. "I want you to think about what you're going to say to the sheriff. If you don't want to lie, it might be best to say nothing and let him come to his own conclusion. After all, if Goran's friends hurt you that badly, then you couldn't have been in on the mine with them."

Nya had stopped eating and was barely breathing as she listened to Yasna. She'd been so happy to know that Yaro was alive that she'd forgotten about all she had left behind. Could the sheriff truly believe she had been roughed up by Goran's friends? "Did Yaro say anything about…how I looked?"

"No. He was asleep in Goran's bed while I cleaned and dressed you and didn't gain consciousness until after I was done, and then he only saw your face above the blanket."

"And you didn't tell him."

"I didn't tell anyone. Even the doctor only saw you from the neck up." She sat back in the chair with a sigh. "Yaromir didn't want to leave you. He said he'd been thinking over some conversations he's had and feels certain that others are involved in the mine. He wants you to go to the sheriff as soon as you can." She caught Nya's gaze. "You're lucky to have him as an advocate. He's a good witness. Well respected and all."

He was *too* good a witness. Fear stabbed Nya's heart. Yaro had nosed around both before and after approaching her about the mine. If powerful people were involved, then he might not survive to give testimony at all. She set the tray aside, tossed off the covers, and stood up. It was time to face the fury.

"Nitty, you're not—"

A wave of dizziness hit her, but she stayed on her feet. "I'm fine." She took a step and frowned. "Do you think you could help me dress?"

"No. You need to eat and—" Yasna halted as a firm knock landed on the door. "Come in!"

The maid entered, her eyes flicking nervously from Yasna to Nya. "The watchmen are here for you."

Nya nodded jerkily. "Tell them to wait in the sitting room."

"They won't come inside. They say you're both to come with them for questioning. Now."

Nya glanced at Yasna, then said, "Tell them we'll be down shortly."

"Yes, ma'am."

With Yasna's help, Nya dressed quickly in a loose-fitting town frock. She glimpsed her pouch in the corner of her wardrobe and scooped it up. She knew she should leave the filthy thing, but it had become so much a part of her over the years that doing so felt like severing a limb. The dark leather hid the worst of the dirt and stains anyway. After donning a clean pair of shoes, they both descended the stairs to the waiting men.

Nya had assumed that she and Yasna could talk in the carriage, but to her surprise the watchmen escorted them to separate carriages. The isolation, together with the look of distaste on the men's faces, rattled Nya. She peered out the window at her receding home. The path that led to Goran's property was cluttered with uniformed men on horseback. What would they find in the outbuilding? Mining tools? Gold? More barrels of poison? She and Yaro should have kicked the door down and had a look inside. Now the sheriff could use her ignorance to his advantage, and Nya wouldn't know truth from falsehood. Her fingers clenched over the pouch. She felt the shape of the crystal shard through it, and for some reason that comforted her.

The courthouse was a white, three-story building that stood on a rocky rise overlooking the town. Its pillared façade and huge double doors were meant to look imposing, though none of it approached the grandeur of the otherworld's round chamber. The carriage pulled up at the steps that led to the great porch. As Nya stepped out, a boy shouted her name. She caught a glimpse of Yaro's young helper before two burly watchmen closed around him and forced him away.

"I want to talk to him," Nya demanded, but her escort laid a firm hand on her arm and tugged her toward the stairs.

She was led into a small, sparsely furnished room with a single curtained window. A slender man with a tidy beard and thinning black hair extended his hand to her. His firm, swift handshake made her wince and then furtively explore her injuries. Why hadn't she thought to wear gloves? He must have noticed, for he eyed her hands with a peculiar intensity. "Nya Stary," he said as she hid her hands behind her back. "I am Sheriff Neclan. How are you?" He smiled, but a tightness around his eyes ruined the effect.

"Tired. Achy."

"Would you like some wine?"

"No. Thanks."

Something in her tone made him lift a dark eyebrow. He waved her to a chair at the table, sat across from her, and dipped a pen into an ink jar. "Why do you think you're here?"

So he would toy with her for a while. She sighed, wishing she could be sure that Yaro was safe. Why had his helper tried to contact her?

"Nya?"

She straightened in the chair. "I wish to speak with Yaromir Korobin."

"Answer my questions first." The nib scraped against the jar's glass rim. "Why do you think you're here?"

"Because of what my brother did to the Witterkin."

"What did he do?"

"You already know that. Yaro was here earlier to give a statement."

"I want to hear it from you."

"He used some sort of poison to kill them so he could get to a cave on the other side."

Pen scratched paper. "Were you in the cave?"

"I was twice, with Yaro. But you already know this."

"What did you see?"

Her lips tightened. "A mass of red Witterkin, some covering my brother and two of his friends. I didn't get a good look at the back of the cave, but one wall looked partly excavated."

"Who were dead, aside from your brother?"

She gave him the names. The pen dipped and scraped. Words formed on the page. He looked at her from the tops of his eyes. "Were there any injuries? Blood?"

She shook her head.

"Who else was involved in the mining enterprise?"

"I don't know."

"When did *you* get involved?"

"I didn't. I had nothing to do with this." Her voice had become strained. She wished she could get up and pace the room, like Yasna had. It would have relieved tension.

The sheriff set his pen down and leaned toward her on the table. "Nya, I know that people don't think well of you. Folk in this town are spiteful and don't mind hurting each other with poisonous gossip, but I want you to know something: I don't care what they say. The only thing that matters to me is the truth, and I will get it. That's what I do, and I'm good at it. So you need to talk to me." He snatched up the pen again and spoke conversationally. "Tell me what happened. Start from wherever you think is best, and give me the whole story."

Nya unclenched her arms and stared at the curtained window. Beginning with the day her father died, she unravelled the whole ugly thing: the change in the Witterkin's voice, her meeting with the lawyer and the division of property, Yaro's conversation with her at the dance, and her subsequent trips to the Witterkin, both alone and with Yaro. She even recounted her conversation with Yasna. He scribbled frantically and only interrupted to ask if someone might have overheard her and Yaro's conversation at the dance. She relaxed into the chair afterward, believing he was done with her. She was wrong.

He turned over a page, dipped the pen, and asked, holding her eyes, "What happened to your hands?"

"I fell on some broken crystal." Both his brows lifted this time, but she added firmly, "It's the truth." She should have wrapped her hands before climbing down that fall of crystal on the mountain. Too many should-haves.

"The item must have been large," he said.

"It was."

"Hmm. I wonder what the doctor will say once he's examined you."

Her breath caught. She tried to keep her face impassive, even as her heart sped up. "Only my hands?"

"No. A full examination will be required."

"I don't wish to be examined."

"I'm afraid you have no choice. Could you repeat your story, please, and this time include everything—every conversation, every meal, every minute you remember, no matter how seemingly unimportant?"

Long hours passed, and Nya found herself hunched over the table, speaking into her folded arms. Some things should have been easier to recall than they were, or at least the sheriff probably thought so. He believed she was relating events from the previous two weeks, but to her these things might as well have happened a lifetime ago. Of course, she kept the otherworld out of her story.

When she finished, he got up and paced the length of the room. Then, without warning, he dragged his chair over to hers and sat on it. "You didn't mention the broken crystal. Those—" he pointed to her hands— "look like defensive wounds. How did you get hurt, Nya?"

She had never felt such a strong urge to leave a room, and yet she remained seated, her eyes meeting his unflinching stare. Perhaps he was right. He *would* dig up the truth. And why shouldn't he? What was the point in hiding from him?

She fumbled with her belt pouch. "I have a shard of the crystal. Kept it on a whim."

There. Let him see what it did—if it did anything at all in this world—and then he would believe her story. Her hands changed the moment she lifted it out of the pouch. She smiled at her long, graceful fingers and shapely nails. Even her wrists looked elegant. The beauty was somewhat marred by her injuries, but her face was unmarked; it must be stunning. She held up the crystal on her open palm.

The sheriff gave it a cursory glance, his eyes betraying only mild interest. "Looks sharp," he commented.

Hadn't he noticed? Hiding it in her palms, she brought it to her neck and pressed it to her skin.

He looked at her and then dipped his pen. "How large was the item that broke, and how did it break?"

Nya couldn't answer. A storm was gathering inside her, sending prickles up her back. "I thought humans couldn't see the effects," Nenad had said. And the sheriff clearly couldn't. That meant only one thing: Nenad had been right. Nya was not, and never had been, fully human.

Something wet trickled down her wrist. The sheriff's chair scraped the floor. He said something, but it was lost in the roaring in her ears. A wave of dizziness struck her, and she lurched forward to vomit her food. It splattered on his paper and pens. Someone shouted, hands gripped her, and she felt herself dragged off into the hallway.

She was behind the barred door of a prison cell when she came back to herself. A man and woman stood over her bed. Doctors, by the look of their smocks and clean white gloves. *Yes,* she thought, *have a good look at the monster.* A chill on her skin told her she had been undressed. Only her underclothes remained. Nya's lips curled back, baring her jutting dogteeth. She hoped it frightened them. "Leave me alone," she warned. But she knew they were only words. She had neither the will nor the energy to fight them.

The male doctor set a large hand on her shoulder. "I'll leave now, and Agata will see to you. Be nice to her. She's just doing her job."

The barred door opened and closed. The male doctor and a guard conferred in low tones for a few moments outside her cell before they both walked off down the hallway. As their steps receded to silence, Agata cleared her throat. "I'm to do a thorough examination."

When Nya didn't answer, she shrugged and launched into it.

Nya grimaced and closed her eyes as she was prodded and pressed. Agata asked her how she had gotten this old injury and that, and Nya always muttered the same thing: she got it while she was in the Witterkin. When Agata parted her legs, Nya lurched up and demanded to know what she was doing.

"Sheriff Neclan asked me to look for evidence of rape. It'll only take a moment."

So, Nya had to lie back and endure one last indignity before the woman finally left, leaving Nya's clothes in a neat pile on the floor. At least they had replaced the bandages. Tears pricked her eyes as she dressed herself. Her pouch was gone and the crystal with it. She curled into a ball on the bed and wished herself into oblivion.

The evening passed into a fitful night. A guard had given her food and water, but she wouldn't touch it in case it was poisoned. She suspected that the watchman tasked with walking the Witterkin fence had been in on the mine. If he had access to the prison, or had friends who did, then Nya might be in danger. He—and anyone else who'd been involved in the mine—didn't know what information Yaro had gathered and had passed to her. Better to get rid of her than risk something coming out. Maybe she was being overly cautious, but better paranoid than dead.

As morning approached, she went from depressed to simply being numb. The challenges she had experienced in the other world made lying in a cell less daunting; even her hunger was nothing new. She had made a conscious decision to stop worrying about Yaro. It was probably best to put a space between them again anyway. Better that than be forced to tell him the truth. A thorn of pain bloomed in her chest.

Not fully human. The fact made the townsfolk's condemnation of her justified, along with her own long-held estimation of herself. She was a freak, plain and simple, and it wouldn't have mattered if she had been more open and friendly; people must know she was a freak on some instinctual level. Even the sheriff's initial friendliness had been put on to gain her confidence.

If only she could return to the other world. Find Nenad and hunt for mudgumps. Her mouth watered as she recalled the buttery, tender flesh. She could almost smell them.

Half a day must have gone by before the sheriff asked to speak to her again. The guard escorted her to the same small chamber as before, but this time a stew pot and a pitcher of water stood on the table. The sheriff waved her to the usual chair, placed an empty bowl and wooden cup—not glass, she noted wryly—in front of her, and then returned to his side of the table. He poured himself some water and scooped stew into his bowl. Nya's hands shook under the table. The smell of the stew was enough to make her dizzy. She waited for him to offer her some or at least to return the scoop to the pot. He did neither.

"Have some water, Nya."

"I will, thank you." She forced her hand still before grasping hold of the pitcher and filling her cup. Then it was as if a silent battle took place. The sheriff eyed her as he lifted his glass, ever so slowly. It paused halfway to his mouth. After an excruciating pause, he downed the water and sat back with a sigh.

Nya drained her cup and poured herself another. The water took the edge off her hunger. She said, "Where is Yaro? His worker wanted to talk to me yesterday."

"Yaro is being held in the most secure cell we possess, for his own safety."

"And he's consented to that?"

"Of course. He isn't suspected of anything, Nya. And he's not the only witness being held in protective custody. There *are* other people involved in this mine. Until we know how dangerous they are, we can't take any chances."

She ran a hand through her messy hair. "What about me? Do I have a choice in being here?"

"No. Until you tell me the truth, I can't rule out your involvement." He lifted a silver spoon and took a swallow of stew. "I want some names from you today, Nya."

"I don't have any." She looked around but could find no spoon.

The sheriff ignored her pointed gestures. "You told me yesterday," he said as he refilled his glass, "that Goran asked you not to go near the Witterkin, but you did anyway, didn't you? And saw something you shouldn't have. So you were hurt. And now you're afraid that those same people will find a way to hurt you again, even here. So you're not eating." He regarded her as he spoke, perhaps gauging her reaction. When she gave him nothing, his lips tightened and his finger tapped the table. "You must tell me the truth, Nya."

"I *have* told the truth. No human caused these injuries. I'll swear to that on anything you want. As for my caution, I think it's warranted, don't you?"

She flinched as he sprang to his feet and grabbed the pot. Nya had to stop herself from reaching for it. Her desperation fed into anger. She shouted, "What else do you want from me? I could lie—"

"You already have." He strode to the door, pot in hand, then turned. "I asked the servants at the Stary manor whether any crystal had gone missing or was smashed. They said no to both. No broken crystal, Nya." He paused as if waiting for her to tell him where he might find the mysterious crystal. When she said nothing, he stalked out of the room, taking the pot with him. Nya was a breath away from grabbing his empty bowl and licking it clean when a guard entered and led her back to her cell.

CHAPTER TWELVE

Yasna

A cell door opened and closed. Yasna wasn't sure if the sound came from her hallway or from another across the building. Sounds echoed strangely in this cold stone structure. She rubbed a knuckle that flared up when she was cold. The flimsy blanket they had given her was a joke. She could keep warm only if she folded it over twice, and then it wasn't long enough to cover her legs. She swore under her breath. What right did they have to hold her in this cell? She hadn't committed a crime, and neither had Nitty.

She went still and then shook her head. What had that poor girl been through anyway? The memory of her lying on the ground in the Witterkin cave made Yasna shudder. Nitty was right. There was only one way she could have come out looking like that—she must have spent days in some otherworld. The fact reordered Yasna's view of reality.

Ever since Yasna had landed in Sundyr, she had tried to fit in. Wear the uncomfortable clothes that were popular here. Set aside her people's "silly" folk tales and embrace reality. She had loosened up a little in recent years and even gained a couple of friends, but perhaps it was time to reassess what she had become. And what stories she had left behind.

Footsteps sounded, growing ever closer. Yasna got to her feet just as a guard inserted the key in the lock and opened her cell door. "Sheriff wants to see you."

The guard led her down three floors to a small room with an open window. Warm evening light streamed in, shining off one of the building's white pillars. As the door closed behind her, a uniformed man she knew as the sheriff greeted her by name and extended his hand, along with an ingratiating smile. She assumed he wanted a handshake. Instead, he took her cold hand in both of his and patted it. "My dear, you've been through quite the ordeal these past few—"

Yasna snatched her hand back. "Don't you dare pat my hand. Touch me again and I'll pitch your skinny ass out the window."

The sheriff's eyes widened. Yasna's gaze flitted around the room. She had gone too far. Still. She rubbed her stroked hand on her clothing. The unwanted touch made her skin crawl.

He cleared his throat and gestured to one of two chairs at a table in the center of the room. "My apologies. Please have a seat. Would you like a glass of wine?"

"No, thank you."

He shrugged and slid into the opposite chair. The man was like a snake, all smooth and glittery-eyed, with no genuine warmth in his body. She itched to be away from him.

He opened a satchel and removed some stationery. "The doctors examined Nya yesterday. They concluded that she was tortured about a week ago, with a variety of implements."

Yasna's stomach clenched, but she said nothing. Doctors could be wrong. Especially when it came to things they knew little about. The Witterkin were among those things.

The sheriff continued, "Miss Stary is still so afraid that she won't eat food brought to her cell, for fear of poison." He opened an ink jar. "We need to find the people who did this to her. If you know anything—"

"I don't. I'm sorry." *Not eating.* How long would this go on for? Nitty was being *too* cautious. The only person at risk of being poisoned was Yaromir. Without him, Nya's testimony would be worthless.

"No matter," the sheriff said. "There may be something you've forgotten or didn't consider important." He dipped his pen. "I want you to go back to the day Nya gave your cat a flea bath and tell me everything she said from then until you found her in the Witterkin."

Her gaze fell to the shiny tabletop. "My memory isn't perfect."

"Do the best you can, please."

She shrugged. Maybe if she did, he would let her see Nitty. She held that thought close to her as she launched into her retelling.

He stopped her at the point when Nitty had first spoken of the red Witterkin. "Did she have any visible injuries then?"

Her lips pursed. "No."

Twice he made her go over their conversations. Of course, he believed that Nitty's injuries had come from enemies in *this* world. Yasna was glad that she'd anticipated this and warned Nitty before the sheriff had gotten to her.

Yasna tensed when she was asked to describe how Yaromir and Nya had looked when she found them. She knew she couldn't lie to him about Nitty's injuries, but clothing was another matter. When asked to describe them, she settled on the vague word, "dirty."

He scratched out a few words, then pinned her with his beady eyes. "I've spoken to the maid. She says you wouldn't allow her in while you dressed and cleaned Nya. Why is that?"

"My preference. I don't like crowding."

"Where did you put the clothes Nya was wearing?"

"They fell to the floor."

"And after that? The maid said she never found them."

When Yasna remained silent, he leaned back and tented his fingers. "An older man lives with you."

Yasna's head jerked up. Worry stirred in the pit of her belly. "Yes. My servant, Tachen."

"Your *servant*."

"What does he have to do with anything?"

"You might have asked him to dispose of certain items. I think I'll bring him in for questioning."

Yasna leapt to her feet. "You don't go near him! He doesn't know anything. And he has a bad heart."

"That may be, but if you won't talk..."

She sat back down, breathing hard. Her own heart was thundering through her. Her voice was small as she said, "Nit-Nya's clothes and boots are in an empty plant pot in her shed."

"Why did you hide them?"

When she didn't respond, he got up and waved her to the door. "Come. We are going to get them, and then you're going to talk."

"Now? It's late." The summer sun had sunk, leaving only a wisp of light.

"Now."

Nya

Darkness had fallen. Another night to be faced alone. Out of curiosity, Nya called out to see if anyone else was imprisoned on the same floor. A distant male voice answered, but she couldn't make out his words. She felt anything but safe as she lay in darkness on the bed. Even though no one could enter her cell, someone could shoot an arrow or throw a knife through the door's bars.

She got up, pushed the bed away from the wall, and lay down behind it on the floor. Tucking the blanket around her, she drifted into a deep sleep.

She woke to the sound of a key turning. Lamplight flared into her cell. Heart hammering, she peered over the edge of her mattress. A guard stood in the doorway. Hooking his lamp over a horizontal bar, he said, "Sheriff wants to see you again."

"Now? It's late."

"It's not yet midnight. Come." He spoke with a lazy drawl, as if he had been drinking.

Nya would give the sheriff an earful, and maybe more. She considered what she would dare to do as she rose stiffly and followed the guard out.

She didn't expect the arm that closed around her neck. As she gasped in a breath, a cloth smelling of soporifics slammed over her face. "I have a knife," the guard warned. "Move or make a sound and I'll kill you, right here and now." Nya froze, her mind reeling. If he wanted her dead, he would already have done it. What did he mean to do with her then? Her lungs began screaming for air. It was either pass out from suffocation or breathe in the fumes. Had she already? Spots of blackness dotted her vision.

She drew a breath through the cloth.

Yaro

Yaro lay in a dim cell in a centuries-old castle dungeon on the outskirts of town. The sheriff had tried to make the space more comfortable by adding a layer of fresh straw to the floor, a feather bed, a chair, and a clean, warm blanket, but it didn't dispel the gloom of the place. Lamplight shining through the bars of his cell door illuminated ancient graffiti on the cell walls. Much of it was nonsense. Dates, names, curses. He closed his eyes and rubbed his face.

He regretted leaving Nya, but he couldn't let the stableman give the only report. The man believed that Yaro had attacked Nya while they were out together—a bizarre notion that the sheriff had eventually dismissed (or at least it appeared he had). But because of the initial suspicion, Yaro had been prevented from speaking to her, even through his helper. For a time, Yaro thought that if he pleased the sheriff enough, he would be allowed to relay a message to her. Instead, the opposite had happened. Every drip of information Yaro gave him seemed to frustrate him more. Through his own digging, Yaro had come to know who was at the periphery of the crime, and this had led him to believe that more than three people were involved. But who were these others? The sheriff wanted more than hearsay and guesswork, which was all Yaro could offer. He wanted evidence, and he'd begun using Yaro's feelings for Nya as leverage to try to shake out information Yaro didn't possess. It had become a painful ordeal.

The only bright spot in the whole affair came from the knowledge that he had healed the Witterkin.

A faint smile came and went on his face. It had been like the moment he knew he'd succeeded in making a crow windstone—the feeling that he had gone beyond what he should be capable of to a place just past the horizon of possibility. He shouldn't have been able to recreate a Witterkin's unearthly voice. But it had happened anyway.

How much of it had Nya witnessed?

Guilt twisted in him as he considered how close she had come to death. He should have known she would follow him into the cave. If Yasna hadn't come by to investigate that morning…

He shuddered and thrust the close call from his mind.

If only Nya were *here* with him now, where he could be sure she was safe. The sheriff believed the castle was more secure than the courthouse. If it was, then why hadn't Nya been brought here? The answer Yaro had gotten—that her life wasn't in danger—hadn't satisfied him, and with no other explanation, Yaro could only conclude that the sheriff, like so many others, cared little for Nya's well-being.

The thought grated on him. Yaro had been aware of the ugly rumors about her throughout the years. His attempts to combat them had failed miserably. Even his helper believed that Nya was cursed.

Of course, her own behavior hadn't helped matters. Nya used to talk his ears off—and the ears of whoever else would listen. And then the accident happened, and she lost that confident spark she'd always carried within her. Yaro regretted that even more than he did killing her mother. At least her mother had lived a full life. It seemed that Nya had been broken before her life could truly begin. People liked to kick broken things, and that was what had happened and continued to happen to Nya.

The sheriff ought to know better than that, though. Yaro would have to speak to him again tomorrow about her transfer.

Yawning, he drew his rough blanket up to his chin and tried to find sleep.

The clang of the food slot wakened him. He sat up, surprised by the brush of daylight in the hallway. His stomach was an angry pit. He retrieved the tray and dove into the porridge. He was about to break the accompanying loaf when he spied a small hole on its underside. Probably a bubble in the batter. *Or maybe not.* Carefully, he broke the loaf in two and held it to the morning light. His breath caught in his throat. A rolled slip of paper had been cooked into the loaf. It cracked when he opened it, but he could still make out the words: *We have Nya. Recant your story and she will live. More when you return home.*

For several moments, he sat frozen to the mattress, staring at the words as if they contained hidden meanings. Then he lurched to his feet and slammed his palm against the bars. The answering pain barely registered. Was Nya in pain? What would they do to her? He opened his hand and stared at the crumpled note. Someone with a fine hand had written it. Not some dumb thug, then, but an educated one.

Return home.

Yes. He would. Hands trembling, he gathered the fragments together and ate them.

When the guard returned for the tray, Yaro demanded to see the sheriff.

He was escorted up a spiral staircase to a modest room in what would have been the old gaoler's quarters. The sheriff was hunched over a desk. A pile of dirty rags and some worn boots lay on the floor by his feet. He looked up when the door opened, revealing shadowed eyes in a stiff face. *He knows,* Yaro thought. *He knows she's gone.* Just as Yaro opened his mouth to recant, the sheriff said, "Nya has been abducted."

Yaro forced himself to look surprised. "How? Who?"

The man regarded him for half a breath before slouching over his desk again. "You're a terrible liar. But that's good to know. It means you weren't lying to me before." He gestured tiredly to a chair by the desk. "Sit down."

Yaro took a step and halted. He was so used to mindlessly obeying the man that he had stopped thinking for himself. Well, that would have to end. If he didn't get the upper hand, the sheriff would ride over his demands as if they had never been voiced. "I prefer to stand," he said, then added, "I don't intend to stay long."

The sheriff ignored the comment. "You were contacted. How?"

Yaro made no reply.

After a long pause, the sheriff approached him, stopping inches from his face. Yaro was taller and better muscled, but he lacked the sheriff's ability to cow someone with a hard stare.

Wind rattled against the window, and a faint whistle escaped. Yaro perked up at the sound. Wind was like a powerful scent to him. It drove everything from his mind, leaving him tense, distracted, and sometimes achingly unfulfilled. But he was glad for it now. As his mind cleared, the sheriff diminished before him. His dark, beady eyes turned to marbles and his frown to a twisted bit of leather. Perhaps the man sensed a change in Yaro, for he merely sniffed and retreated to his desk. He spoke as he straightened one of the worn boots that had fallen over. "You are withholding the information we need to find her."

"I'm not staying in this place anymore. I recant everything I said. No one else was involved in the mine, and those that were are dead. I'll make no statement in court to the contrary."

The sheriff opened the desk drawer, removed a bottle of brandy and a glass, and poured himself a shot. "They won't kill her," he said, almost conversationally. "If she dies, her property goes to the state, and the state no longer sells land that holds Witterkin. But if she lives, there's still a chance they can secretly work the mine. All they'd have to do is threaten her—or perhaps Yasna—and she would give in and let them do it."

"What about the Witterkin?"

He shrugged. "Poison did the trick before, and it will again. If they have enough poison and a watchman willing to take a bribe, they're set. At least in the short term. But depending on the gold deposit, they might not need a great deal of time." He tossed back the brandy, cleared his throat, and then poured himself some more. "If you leave here, they'll kill you. They know you were digging for information a few days ago, and if they've contacted you, it means they know you're here instead of at the courthouse, and if you're here, they can only assume that you're an important witness. Do you see the logic?"

"I'm not stupid."

"Good. Then you'll do the smart thing and stay here. Let us find her."

Yaro shook his head. He would not gamble Nya's life on the sheriff's assurances. And he wasn't completely helpless. "I'm leaving," he said firmly.

The sheriff pressed his hand down hard on the top of the glass. Then he crossed the room and flung open the door. "Go then. I'll arrange a carriage to take you back into town."

Yaro turned at once and left the room. He had to wait half an hour before his belongings were returned to him, then a guard escorted him out of the castle and up a path to the gate. Yaro felt watched with every step. And of course, he was, and would continue to be long after he left the castle. The only reason the sheriff had let him go was in hopes that Yaro would lead him to the criminals. But Yaro couldn't allow that. He wouldn't be allowed to find Nya while being flanked by trailing watchmen. He would have to lose them.

Sunlight hit him as he stepped outside the gate and got into the waiting carriage.

CHAPTER THIRTEEN

Nya

Nya woke slowly, her weary mind weaving in and out of colorful dreams. Nenad's high-pitched voice played through them all, singing a Lake Lady song, and then a Fabric song. Then the Lake Lady again. His last words before she opened her eyes stayed with her: *May you find peace in the warp and weft of the world.*

Not in this world, she thought.

She lay on a hard, uneven surface. A rising wall of damp stone loomed over her head. Her arms ached under her back, and her hands were numb. She tried to wrench them out, only to find that her wrists were bound together. She shifted onto her side and winced as the blood streamed back into her hands. Her ankles were trussed so tightly that the rope chafed her skin. She tested the bindings and found them strong.

Her sticky eyes took in her surroundings. She was in a bottle-shaped cave with the wider end at the back. Weeds grew along the walls and in cracks in the floor. Water dripped nearby, but the sound didn't echo. The cave's entrance, which she estimated to be forty feet away, was an empty circle of glaring white light. The brightness hurt her eyes and created deep shadows in the cave walls.

As she drew breath to scream for help, a murmur of voices came to her from the direction of the cave entrance. Nya strained to hear the soft words.

"No, I won't allow it," a woman hissed. Nya froze in shock at the familiar voice.

"Why?" a man whined. "Why do you care either way?"

"Because we need her alive and healthy."

"It won't kill her. She might even enjoy it. I'd wager she's never had any, being a witch and all."

"You ignorant little shit. If you knew anything about women, you wouldn't say that."

The voices lowered to angry whispers, but they had spoken long enough for Nya to be sure of them both. Nya's captors were Faina and her brother, Mirko.

Faina, the simpering, delicate woman who used to cringe whenever Goran swore, even if it was under his breath. She must have been involved in the mine; perhaps she had even been the one to convince Goran to open it. Nya well remembered her recent visit. Faina had made such a fuss about Goran's disappearance that Nya had let her rummage around the Stary home. She hadn't been looking for him. Likely, she had raked through his belongings in search of incriminating evidence. Had her satchel looked heavier afterward? Nya had been so distracted by the woman's tears that she hadn't noticed. Faina's visit to Goran's outbuilding had probably been more of the same: searching, stealing.

It was all an act. Had Faina cared about Goran at all, or had the relationship been based on greed rather than on genuine love for him? Nya was almost grateful that her brother wasn't around to find out.

She brought her knees up to her chest and shivered. If her hands hadn't been bound behind her, she might have chewed her bindings or searched for a rock to use as a weapon. As it was, she could scarcely move at all. At least they wanted her alive for the moment. She moved her tongue around in her mouth, trying to create some moisture. She felt sick with hunger and thirst. In the past three days, she'd had one breakfast and a glass of water. She wondered if the lack of food was fogging her mind, or if the soporifics used on her were at fault. Probably the soporifics. Her thoughts had not been this muddled in the prison cell.

She stiffened as a shadow emerged from some sort of recess in the rock wall. "She's awake," Faina said.

"I can—"

"No, you stay here. Keep an eye on the opening."

In a few steps, Faina was at Nya's side. She held a flask to Nya's mouth and let her drink the ice-cold water.

"More," Nya said as her captor pulled the flask away.

"Maybe later." Faina sat back on her haunches. She wore a woollen cape with a large hood shadowing her face. Her tall boots fit snugly to her legs, but the leather creaked as she squatted, rendering them more fashionable than practical in a situation such as this. Did she believe this costume would conceal her identity? Nya loosed a soft snort. "Why are you doing this to me, Faina?"

The girl sighed and laid a hand on Nya's shoulder. "I'm sorry, but it's the way it has to be. You see, Goran and I were in this together—"

"This?"

"The mine. Don't pretend to be ignorant. You know what he did, and the income it would have created. Did you really think he chose that land by the mountain on a whim?"

"I–I wasn't thinking clearly then."

"No, and neither was he. Goran should have brought you into this sooner, but he wouldn't listen to me." She paused, tilting her head. "What did you tell the sheriff?"

Nya hated herself for speaking so humbly to this woman, but she couldn't afford to make an enemy of her. Not when she was Nya's only defence against Mirko. And, she added to herself, whoever else might assault her. Where was the guard who had abducted her from the prison cell? She replied, "Just what I saw."

"And heard?" Faina shifted closer. "What names did you give him?"

"Only those that belonged to the three corpses."

"Good." Her nails bit into Nya's shoulder. "You know, Goran loved us both, and he wouldn't have wanted us to suffer because of his actions. He had a future planned for us, Nya. If we let it slip away, then he'll have died for nothing. So stay strong, and when all this is over, we can move forward again. All right?" She let go of Nya's shoulder. Her boots creaked as she stood up.

"You never answered my question," Nya said. "Why am I here? What's happening? If you want to bring me into this, then start now."

Faina paused and then continued on to the recess in the wall. Her heels made soft tapping sounds on the stone floor. "Just wait a bit longer. It'll all be over soon."

Nya struggled to sit up. "I'm hungry."

"You'll survive. Just wait a bit longer."

Yaro

The guards were silent during the journey from the castle to Yaro's old manor house, refusing to answer any questions Yaro put to them. He wondered, as he stepped down from the carriage, which one of the two guards would remain behind to shadow him. No matter. After a swift scan of his property, he jogged up the cobbled path to the door and lifted the knocker. The hounds bayed before his manservant opened the door. Yaro knelt and buried the animals' sleek heads in his chest, muttering nonsense words.

"Did anything happen while I was away, Wenden?" Yaro asked, trying to keep his voice casual.

"Yes, sir. Someone slipped a note for you under the door. I have it here..."

Yaro accepted the folded page and broke the plain wax seal. "The same handwriting," he murmured as he read, trying to steady his hands. He leaned against the closed door with a shuddering breath. They had given him Nya's location. He knew how he would get to it, but it would be challenging to approach the spot without being seen.

One of his hounds whined. Yaro reached around it and locked the front door. "I'll be in the weapons chamber and then in the cellar, Wenden. If anyone comes by, do not open the door. It might be best to arm yourself in case someone comes through a window."

Wenden's eyes widened, but he merely nodded and said, "Yes, sir." Yaro wasn't surprised by his lack of fear. Wenden's forebears had been employed by the Korobins for two centuries, and they had all been trained to defend themselves if need be. Wenden was no exception.

"Sir..."

Yaro paused in the hallway and looked back at his slender, middle-aged servant. "Yes?"

"Your father had a pair of soft-soled shoes. They might serve you well during your...time in the cellar."

Several moments passed before Yaro could frame a response. He had never heard of such shoes, and he had been all through his father's things. "They might indeed. Where would I find them?" Fortunately, he and his father had shared the same shoe size.

"In the cellar, sir."

"Of course. Thank you."

"Would you like me to pack you some provisions? The cook is out at the moment."

"No. I'll do it myself. Keep watch for me, Wenden. And mind what I said about danger."

Yaro left him in the entryway and continued on down the hallway to a door that led to a spiral staircase mainly used by the servants. At the first landing, he paused and unlocked a sturdy oaken door.

The chamber he entered was visited by very few people, yet it took up a good half of the manor's second floor. Sunlight poured in from its two large windows, illuminating a long, unbroken wall covered by weapons. Most had belonged to his ancestors, but Yaro had added a few of his own throughout the years—a dagger made of windstone, slitted in its center, a crossbow made of black yew, a slender spatha, and a double-edged two-handed sword. Several complete suits of armor were also on display, each standing upright on wooden dummies.

It was a formidable sight. To Yaro however, it was familiar, if not nostalgic. The Korobins had kept their passion for arms and armor a secret to all but their most trusted servants (the weapon smiths had been sworn to secrecy). One of their ancient ancestors had been a king's champion, and even after the Korobins veered away from this occupation, they considered their battle skills a matter of family pride. Yaro had practiced with his father as a boy and continued that training into adulthood. However, after his father's death, he'd been too busy to spare it much time. Now he wished he had.

His hands trembled a little—as much, he thought wryly, from excitement as from dread—as he wrapped his forearms in leather and secured a belt to his waist. He eyed the armor longingly. A full suit would be useless for stealth, but he might get away with a cuirass if he wore a shirt over it. And a helmet.

He spent a good hour on target practice and a further half hour sharpening his blades before heading down to the pantry.

The manor was as silent as a tomb. Even Wenden's steps were too soft to be audible. Yaro ate without tasting his food, then padded to his own chamber to shrug on a loose-fitting shirt. Throughout all this, he struggled not to think about Nya. Even if the sheriff was right about her captors wanting her alive, it said nothing about how they would treat her. In fact, if their goal was to subjugate, then they would have every reason to break her, by whatever means their imaginations could conjure.

He forced himself to loosen his clenched jaw. When he opened the cellar door, he was armed with an ankle knife, a short sword, and a crossbow. His arrows were arranged so they wouldn't rustle together when he walked. His nasal helm was smooth to his head.

He felt at once powerful and profoundly vulnerable. He had never intentionally killed someone. The idea seemed straightforward—just aim and shoot. But how would it be when the moment came? Would his hands grow unsteady? Would he hesitate, giving his opponent an opening?

The whole thing could go horribly wrong. In some ways, it was like taking a step in the dark, hoping one's foot would land on solid ground.

He descended the ancient stone steps and ducked to avoid bumping the low ceiling. His small lamp illuminated orderly shelves and wine racks. At the back wall, he set the light down and heaved a rack away. A bottle of elderberry wine smashed on the floor, filling the space with flowers. The scent reminded him so much of his father that he almost turned his head to see if the man stood there.

He felt along the wall behind the rack until his fingers brushed an old latch. The door creaked open, revealing a roughly hewn space, the walls streaked with mineral deposits. The ancient smugglers' tunnel had been built long before the Korobins had purchased the manor. Yaro had caught his father sneaking into it during the last year of his life. The man's mind had failed him, causing him to wander like a lost lamb. Wenden had already known about the tunnel—a fact that had only worsened Yaro's hurt feelings at being excluded. Now, as he stared at the dusty pair of shoes sitting just within the entrance, he felt that pain again. Wenden must have placed them there while Yaro's father's personal effects were being hauled away. Perhaps he thought they belonged with the tunnel. Why neither he nor Yaro's father had seen fit to share these secrets with Yaro was a mystery—one that would doubtless continue to bother him.

The soles were indeed soft. His throat felt tight and his arms heavy as he pulled them on. The leather laces were stiff, but he managed to tie them.

He picked up the lamp and stood awkwardly. A faint whooshing sound reverberated down the dark space. Yaro's steps were silent as he followed it.

Nya

Nya must have drifted off again. She woke as a strong hand slammed over her face, covering her mouth and nose. Panic surged through her. She couldn't breathe, not even to scream. Someone forced her roughly onto her back and straddled her, putting pressure on her bound hands. Nya struggled to make a sound, but all she managed was a muffled moan.

"Mirko?" Faina's sleepy voice from the recess made the man go still. Boots squeaked and small stones shifted. "What are you doing?"

The hand came away, and Nya gasped for air. Hot breath smelling of vodka and cured meat tickled her ear. "Later," he promised and squeezed her breast as he got off her.

Nya screamed, again and again, until her throat was raw.

Faina dropped down beside her. "Screaming won't work here, Nya. Did he hurt you?"

Nya couldn't speak. Her whole body trembled, and her throat was full of acid. She had not felt such a deep fear before, even when she thought she would die after falling into the fissure.

Faina sighed. "Mirko is good with a sword, but that's about all." She pressed a small, hard object into Nya's hand. "If he touches you again, tap this stone against the rock and I'll come."

Nya's fist clenched around the stone. Faina watched her for a moment longer before returning to the recess. Harsh, whispered voices drifted over, then silence descended once more. Nya sought calm, but all she could think about was when she would be attacked again. Faina couldn't always protect her. Even if the woman was awake and alert, Mirko might break free from her hold on him. In truth, it was only a matter of time. And now that Mirko viewed Nya as a helpless victim, she doubted she would ever be truly safe from him again, no matter what came of this sordid affair.

She squeezed her eyes shut and fixed her mind on her peaceful dream of Nenad singing his songs. Even in the worst situations, the chima's simple beliefs usually calmed him.

The wind rose, breathing cool, damp air into the cave.

And something else…

At first, she recognized it only as a voice, but as the wind strengthened and it grew louder, she knew it to be *her* voice. Her breath caught, and her muscles went rigid. The sound rose and fell with the wind. It was a windsong. *Her* windsong.

And with that revelation, she knew where she was: Cape Strach. No other place along the coast held sea caves. The cave Yaro had spoken about all those years ago must be near. She shook her head. He had made her a windstone after all. The fact should have angered her. Perhaps it would have had the voice he made been girlish, but this one belonged to a woman. And it was a shout. A full-blooded war cry tossed out into the world. No wonder Faina had warned her that screaming would be useless. Was this how Yaro had perceived her?

Perhaps he had been right. Perhaps that voice had always been inside her, suppressed. A shiver went through her, and she brought her knees to her chest. The wind rose again, a gust so powerful that Nya felt it on her face. The voice followed it, its tone deepening, like a gathering power. The sound seemed to climb into her skull.

Something deep inside her shifted then, lifted its head like an animal sniffing the wind. It was the same part of her that had sensed the greenshifter's power. But it had been small then, a whisper. Now it reared up and shook itself through her. Her whole body jolted. Her teeth chattered, and she moaned. Footsteps sounded, and someone touched her head. The weight of a blanket settled over her. It did nothing to stave off the chill that had settled into her bones. Something cold and wet touched her lips. She tried to drink, but the water went everywhere. The inside of her mouth tasted like blood. She heard murmured voices and then nothing more. Darkness enfolded her, pulling her down into unconsciousness.

Yaro

Yaro had walked the length of the tunnel before, so he knew he would find himself in the basement of a derelict warehouse when he emerged. The door was so stiff that he was forced to kick it down. The warehouse stood by an old dock on the side of Sundyr opposite Cemetery Hill. Most cargo ships were larger now than they had been when the dock was built, requiring deeper water, so little by little this dock had fallen to disuse.

Yaro mounted the basement's uneven stone stairs and paused at the top, wincing at what the light pouring through the warehouse's busted windows revealed. The empty building had been left to rot. The floorboards sagged in the center, some so dark and pitted that they looked more like earth than wood. The planks near the wall were in better shape than those at the center, but not by much. Cautiously, he made his way along the wall toward the building's broken doors. He flinched when he encountered a soft board and went on even more slowly, testing his weight with each step.

When he was only a handful of yards from the front wall, sudden movement startled him. He looked up to find an old man clutching a ratty blanket and an empty vodka bottle. "Have mercy," the man pleaded in a hoarse voice.

Yaro raised his empty hands. "I mean you no harm."

The man gave a jerky nod and edged away from the door. With a murmur of thanks, Yaro hurried from the building.

The sun was low. He had spent too much time at home before coming here. Turning, he headed for a rocky arm of land that jutted into the sea. Cape Strach was part of what made Sundyr a harbor. From a distance, it truly looked like a bent, sheltering arm, but up close, it was a cold, windy space of slippery stones and bird droppings. The warehouse was nestled in the cape's armpit. Yaro located the remains of an old path and followed it up the cape's rocky slope. Then he dropped to a squat and stared out toward the cape's end. The distant outline of an abandoned lighthouse beckoned him. The building stood in front of a path that led down to some sea caves. The lighthouse would be a perfect spot for an archer to lie in wait. He would expect Yaro to take the direct path toward the sea caves. What other way was there?

Yaro wiped the cold sweat from his brow. He wished he had explored the cape better. The smugglers' caves had long been abandoned, and years of wind and waves had torn stones away from the cliff ledge into the ocean. When Yaro had set Nya's windstone, he had not bothered to explore, choosing instead the most direct route to the caves. He shifted his weight. It was either brave the possible archer's attack head-on or come at him from the side. Both presented dangers.

Wind brushed his neck, and he turned to find a dark cloud bearing down on Cemetery Hill. Though it was far away, he fancied he could hear the raised voices of the dead. He couldn't single out Nya's windsong yet, but he would as he neared the cape's end. Perhaps it would dampen the sound of his approach. "Go slowly," he breathed. Veering off the path, he made for the cape's sloping edge. An unearthly light hung over the scattered stones and tough weeds interspersed among them. After a time, he glanced over the edge to find dark waves instead of sand. The deep, restless ocean now waited, its breath slicking the rocks. He swallowed tightly and took another step.

Nya

Nya couldn't tell if she was awake or asleep. Exhaustion had caused this sort of confusion once before, but this felt different. Had they drugged her again? She lay still, her eyes half-closed and her breathing deep and steady. Gradually, she became aware of two leaves under her head. How had she missed them? They were tough, stringy things that needed little light and even less water. Thoughtlessly, she traced them down to their lengthy stem—a crooked, fibrous cord covered in green fuzz. The roots were deep and wandering. So many pathways through the stone. The cave floor had seemed solid, but the stone was fragile, its surface layered, and seamed with thin cracks. Plants nudged through them, their roots tangled together in spots. But unlike snarled boot laces, these needed no untangling. They were content just to be. She lingered with them a while, then gradually withdrew her focus back to her body.

Her eyes widened, and she knew she had not been dreaming. Somehow the fierce voice of her windsong had awakened something inside her. But whatever it was didn't feel wrong. If anything, it felt like a fuller development of an ability she already possessed.

She shifted uncomfortably under the blanket. Her body was slick with sweat, and she felt as if she had run a mile. But while she was weaker physically, her earlier panic had passed, and she felt oddly at peace. Perhaps the knowledge that she could make her mind go elsewhere had eased her fear of being hurt.

Not human, a small voice reminded her. Maybe even less so now than before. But what did it matter?

Time was when she would have cared. That time had now passed. She moved her head toward the cave's entrance. An unusually beautiful sunset burned in the empty sky.

Mirko's low voice drifted toward her from the recess. "It's getting dark. I told you he wouldn't come tonight, but you wouldn't listen. You never listen."

"Shhh," Faina hissed. "Someone's on the ledge. It's probably just Artem, but you never know."

Mirko drew his sword and stepped into the warm light. Faina left him and crossed to Nya.

"Water," Nya pleaded.

"Later."

As Nya drew breath to beg, a gag was forced against her mouth and secured behind her head. "Shhh. Just a little longer," Faina said. Nya wanted to kick her in the face.

Booted footsteps fell, and a man armed with a crossbow stepped into the cave. He said, "He hasn't left his house yet."

Faina swore, and Mirko threw her an angry glance. Nya was almost certain the archer was the guard who had abducted her from the cell. The build was right, and he spoke with the same lazy drawl.

He unshouldered his quiver. "Nela hasn't moved. She says she'll wait until it's fully dark, and then there's no point in hanging around there."

Faina straightened from her crouch beside Nya. "The target will need a lamp if he comes in the dark. Won't that make him an easy shot?"

"An easy shot," the archer agreed, "but not an accurate one. Besides, there's a storm brewing. Wind makes arrows drift."

Mirko snorted. "You can't carry a light on the cape, anyway. The wind will put it out. No, it's like I said: he isn't coming tonight."

Faina's shoulders slumped, and she looked away from them to the cave's empty opening. The tables were turning on her. Nya could feel it. Mirko was using her poor judgment as a weapon against her. Soon, he would question her other decisions, including her prohibition against hurting Nya.

And there was a long, dark night ahead.

"Do we have enough food?" the archer asked.

Mirko hunched into the shadowy recess. A bottle clinked. "Not really, but we'll have to make do. I'm not about to fetch anything with this storm coming."

Once more, the words seemed aimed at his sister.

The two men settled into the recess, leaving Faina with her hostage. Nya stared at the cave opening. Anyone who entered now would only see Nya and Faina. The others were completely hidden. So, Nya was the bait. But for whom?

Worry pricked her. It could not be Yaro. He was in a secure cell, not at home. Who were they after then? The sheriff?

The wind rose, and her windsong roared over the water. Nya stretched her mouth, trying to shift the gag from where it bit into her skin. She was so weary, so tired of lying in one place while being chafed by ropes. *Time to go elsewhere for a while.*

She let her attention seep back into the leaves under her head.

Once again, knowledge of the wiry plant spilled into her: survival tactics, ways not to merely exist, but to thrive. Just as roots could push through narrow cracks, the stalks could move to follow the sun, not swiftly like the greenshifter's vines, but with strength and purpose nonetheless. She explored that force, giving herself time to fully grasp it. All the while, some instinct urged her to do more than understand, but to become. To *be* that strong little life stretching toward water and sunlight. What would happen if she did?

She set aside her fears and sank deeper until she sensed air on her leaves, cool stone on her roots, and it didn't feel foreign or wrong. Wonder moved through her. In a thought, she could bend this plant to her will. It would be as easy moving her own arm.

After what seemed an endless moment, she drew back from the tranquil darkness into her own flaccid body. Straight away, all her aches and pains returned. She resisted groaning aloud. So, she had discovered a new ability. What good would it do her?

"Shut up, Nya," the archer muttered, making her stiffen. It took her a moment to realize his playful shout wasn't directed at her, but at her windsong.

Mirko chuckled and said quietly, "She's angry because she's never had a man."

"Are you sure about that? I know of a few who go to her for herbs. Maybe they pay her in other ways..."

Before Mirko could reply, a female voice sounded from outside the cave. "Help. Been shot."

The response from the two men was dramatic. The archer scrambled to his feet and snatched up his bow and quiver. Mirko was close behind with a drawn sword.

"Where are you?" the archer inquired.

"Up here. The man's dead."

"Are you sure?"

"Yes."

Mirko hissed out a relieved sigh. The archer lowered his bow and jogged to the ledge.

"Stop!" Faina shouted.

The archer kept walking, but Mirko slowed and threw his sister a questioning glance.

"Why?"

"Because that's not Nela." Her hand trembled as it shifted to a slight bulge at her hip. A blade? Nya wondered.

"Who else would it be?" Mirko demanded.

"I don't know, but I know Nela, and that's not her."

The archer disappeared around the corner. Mirko took a step to follow and then paused again, indecision writ plainly on his features. A heavy thud from outside the cave made both siblings jump. Faina's hand dove into her cape. Nya didn't see the blade she drew, but an instant later she felt its chill against her neck.

Faina's breath tickled the hair at Nya's ear. "Don't move."

It was a stupid thing to say. What could Nya do when she was bound and gagged on the floor? Her eyes fixed on the fiery light outside the cave. A terrible suspicion gripped her heart. She knew only one person who could convincingly mimic another person's voice. He used to make Nya laugh at dances by imitating other people. The ability served him well when determining which tone a client wanted from a windstone.

Yes, it had to be Yaro. Her captors were hunting the Windsinger. Her mind reeled as the horrible reality sank in.

Mirko edged along the wall toward the entrance, his sword raised. "We have Nya," he shouted. "Come out now or we'll slit her throat."

Nya clenched the tiny stone so hard, it bit into her hand. She wished with all her heart that Yaro would just go away. Faina and Mirko had no reason to kill her. If Yaro hadn't risen to their bait, they would eventually have dragged her back home to whatever abuse awaited. But she would have taken it in exchange for Yaro's life. Gladly.

There was a long silence. Nothing indicated that Yaro was coming, no footsteps or creaking of leather boots. And yet suddenly he was there. Or someone was. The warrior's face was partly concealed by a battle helm, and his chest seemed overly wide to be Yaro's. Nya's anxiety eased, but only for an instant.

Then Yaro's deep voice sounded through the helm. "The sheriff and his men are on the cape. If you kill either of us, they'll try you for murder."

Mirko stiffened. He shot his sister a swift, nervous glance.

"He's bluffing," Faina said.

"I'm—" Yaro began.

"What happened to the archers?" Mirko demanded.

When Yaro didn't respond, Faina shouted, "Answer him or I'll kill her!"

"They're dead."

Mirko sucked in an angry breath. "Drop your weapons. And remove your helm so we know it's you. Now!"

Yaro's head bent forward in a nod.

Blood thundered in Nya's ears. This was really happening. They were going to slaughter him in front of her. And he knew it. He knew.

Time seemed to slow. Hardly breathing, she watched him toss his crossbow at the floor by Mirko's feet.

She should fight. Wasn't that what Yaro had planned to do, his own way?

Her eyes closed, and she let the stone fall from her hand. So she would, then. Her own way.

She dove into the plant beneath her head.

Too fast. A feeling of deep disorientation washed over her. For a time, she wandered in the roots like a swimmer in a dark sea, unable to find the surface. Gradually, she forced herself to calmness, and the world settled around her, made sense once more. She flowed from plant to plant, hoping she moved in the right direction. She had spied a sizable weed along the wall near Mirko. If she was right, it would have a large root system.

So many trailing chaotic paths. And she was running out of time. She came to an unusually fat root and let herself seep into it, deeper and deeper, until she shared its senses. She isolated its ability to follow light and changed it, made it her own. The stalk twitched and then shifted, sinking from the wall to the floor.

After it had crawled a few inches, it met an obstacle. If this was the right plant, the barrier should be Mirko's leg. She abandoned the stalk and shot back into her body, following a thin thread of awareness. Dizziness struck her. She blinked as the world settled, and she focused on the man standing near the cave entrance.

A leaf now grazed Mirko's ankle. Thankfully, he hadn't noticed the touch through his boot. Like his sister, his attention was fixed wholly on Yaro, who was now bereft of his quiver, dagger, sword, and helm. She had run out of time. Breathless with fear, Nya returned to the plant. One twist around the ankle, another needed to secure it, and then...

Pain forced her back to her body. *No.*

"Let her go!" Yaro shouted.

A biting pressure at her neck eased a little. Faina said something, but Nya didn't hear it. She was fully in the roots again, rushing back to the large weed. Just as she found it, something wrenched the stalk, snapping off roots. Nya reeled at the damage and then struggled to break free.

Crushing defeat moved through her.

She had failed to snare Mirko, and now it was too late. She could do nothing at all.

CHAPTER FOURTEEN

Nya resurfaced just as a scream rang in her ears. The knife at her neck had shifted higher and was once more cutting into her skin. Warm fluid dribbled over her collarbone. She blinked, trying to understand what she was seeing.

Mirko lay face-down on the cave floor. It seemed that he had tripped and fallen. She'd thought he had noticed the stalk and wrenched it off his ankle. Why wasn't Yaro doing anything now? Why wasn't anyone?

Faina's desperate cry pierced her ears again. "Help him!"

"Let go of her first," Yaro demanded. "You're killing her."

Nya had never seen his eyes so wide and panicked. Was she bleeding that badly? Her neck felt warm and almost numb, though she still sensed the pressure of the blade on it.

"Help him," Faina pleaded again.

Yaro didn't respond. He seemed incapable of moving, his terrified eyes fixed on the blade under Nya's chin.

She made a small, strangled sound, and Faina jerked, dropping the knife. Yaro dashed toward them, snatched up Faina's knife, and cut Nya's gag. He used the cloth to bind her neck wound. All the while, his large hands trembled against her skin.

"I'm all right," Nya said. "Just a few more cuts. What about Mirko? You should disarm him, before he—"

"He's dead," Yaro whispered as he sliced the ropes from her wrists and ankles. "Is the cloth on your neck too tight?"

Nya didn't answer. Her mouth had slackened as she watched Faina turn Mirko onto his back. An angry slash cut him from collarbone to ear; blood streamed from it like a dark river. His lifeless hand still gripped the bloodied sword he had fallen on. Faina closed her hands over the wound, as if to hold the blood in. But it was too late. Far too late.

Without a word, Yaro rose and crossed to the body. His hair was a wild pony mane, tugged in every direction by the wind. Faina didn't seem to notice him, or perhaps she did and didn't care. He paused as if to adjust something on his boot, but when he straightened, the weed was no longer on Mirko's ankle. The movement had been so quick and offhanded that Nya wouldn't have noticed it if she had not been observing him so closely.

He knows, she thought. Somehow, he had seen the vine close around Mirko's ankle and had let it happen. And if he'd taken the time to remove the evidence in such a sneaky way, then he must have guessed the truth.

Her quivering eyelids closed. It was too much. Mirko's unexpected death. Yaro's awareness that she had caused him to fall, and how. She curled her knees into her chest and pushed her face into her hands.

Someone touched her head. "Nya?"

"I'm fine," she said, blinking. She must have blacked out. "Just tired."

Yaro sighed. "I don't know what to do. I can't leave you here while I fetch a doctor; it's not safe. I could carry you, but—no, don't try to stand."

"Too late." She gripped the rock wall as she struggled to her feet. Blackness hovered at the edges of her vision. "I can move on my own. And I'm not staying in this place another minute."

***

They walked into a windy twilight, a sobbing Faina in front, followed by Nya and Yaro. Nya felt better after eating and drinking from her captors' meager store in the recess. Nevertheless, she took her time along the narrow ledge, refusing to look down at the angry waves. Yaro was so close behind that the toe of his boot grazed her heel a couple of times. Her windsong shouted behind them, its voice strengthening in the wild gusts. Worried that she would catch a chill, Yaro had given her his tunic. The shiny armor he wore beneath it had startled her. A loan from the sheriff, she had guessed. But when she'd asked how he had come by it, he'd said simply, "It's mine."

So many secrets, she thought.

At last, they reached the lighthouse and continued on up the old path that led away from it.

Nya glanced back, squinting at the brilliant light from his hand lamp. "Thank you," she said.

A wry grimace tugged on his lips. "For what? My dismal attempt at saving you?"

"For giving me a strong voice. I didn't expect that."

He looked down as if ashamed. "Did it help?"

She tilted her head, wondering if a hidden meaning lurked in those words, but his expression was unreadable. "Just a bit."

"I know you didn't want that windstone made, but I was a stupid kid then, used to getting my own way."

She slowed so they walked side-by-side. "It helped. Sometimes we do the right thing without knowing why we should do it. You were right to make that windstone."

Their hands bumped, and despite all that had happened, warmth filled her. Yaro still valued her, no matter what he had seen in the cave.

The rain came, and they trudged on in silence toward the flickering lights of town.

***

Two days later, Nya sat in the hallway of the courthouse, running her hand over an old knot in the wooden bench. She had not been allowed to speak to Yaro since the night they had reported what happened. Nya had left out the part about the crawling weed. In her story—and doubtless Yaro's—Mirko had simply tripped and fallen on his sword.

Perhaps he had, in reality. She didn't know and almost didn't care. How many had died now because of this sordid affair? The Witterkin had taken three, Yaro the two archers; Mirko made six. Six people, killed for no good reason. It was a lot of death for a small town like Sundyr. Yaro would be busy when he got back to his workshop...

"Hello, Nya." The sheriff's tired voice echoed off the hallway's cold stone walls. He wore his usual freshly pressed uniform, and his salt-and-pepper beard had been moulded to a fine point.

Nya replied with a small hand wave. She had developed a tolerance for the wily man, much as some people acquired a tolerance for poison—with small doses and much discomfort.

He asked, "How are you?"

"Fine."

He sat down on the bench next to her and dropped an open sack of dirty rags on the floor. Nya's nose wrinkled at the stench wafting from it, but she didn't ask why he carried it with him. For all she knew, it was evidence to be used in court.

He drew some folded sheets from his satchel and passed them to her. "This is your witness statement. The judges will receive their own copies, so please read out exactly what is written when it's time to take the stand."

She nodded absently as she scanned the account, holding the pages up so she wouldn't have to bend her head forward. Her bandaged neck wounds were still sensitive. "You have a good memory. Nothing has been left out."

His mouth stiffened in a sour line. "Oh, plenty has been left out, but even a torn net can catch fish." He nudged the sack of rags toward her with the toe of his boot. "This is yours."

"That? No, you must be mistaken."

He shook his head. "There's no mistake. These are the things you wore on the day you were pulled from the Witterkin. Both your stableman and maid confirmed you had them on, though they were clean and whole when you set out that day." His voice trailed on an odd note.

Nya refolded the sheets of paper and rolled them slowly between her hands. "I see." It was all she could manage. Had she truly worn such filthy rags? She fingered her healing belly, remembering the countless bloodstains and all the blemishes she had not been able to remove in river water. Yes, she supposed she had been that soiled.

"Your pouch is in there too," he went on, "with the crystal shard inside it." He cleared his throat and stood.

"Thank you," she said, then added, "I'm sorry you couldn't find the truth you were searching for."

A ghost of a smile played on his lips. "Who says I didn't?"

***

Light streamed from the courtroom's tall leaded glass windows as Nya was escorted in. Sunlight usually cheered her, but these bright pillars felt lofty and glaring. The robed judges in their high seats at one end of the hall echoed the loftiness of the pillars.

On the sheriff's advice, Nya wore a demure town frock and white gloves that hid her healing cuts. The sheriff had sent a guard to fetch them for her from the Stary manor. As she was led to a worn spot on the floor below the judges, her gaze strayed to the prisoners' booth at the opposite end of the hall. Faina was there, clothed in rough wool and shackled in heavy irons. Next to her stood a man Nya recognized as Dren, the watchman tasked with walking the length of the Witterkin every six months. He had also been one of Goran's best friends. If others were involved in the mine, they hadn't been caught.

Both prisoners regarded Nya with narrowed eyes and pinched lips. What if Goran had lived? Would he have stood there too, watching her with contempt? A shiver went through her, almost like pain. Yes, he would. He would have deemed her testimony a betrayal, and any familial loyalty left between them would have dissolved, as if it had never been.

Tears pricked her eyes, and she forced herself to turn away, to put the accused behind her. Goran was dead, along with his plan. There was no point in mulling over what might have happened had he lived.

The sheriff, who stood to one side and lower than the judges, introduced her, and then the high-and-mighty ones indicated that she may read her statement.

A silence fell. Nya loosed an unsteady breath, unfolded the pages, and began to read. Her voice started off unsteady but gained in strength as she described her journey with Yaro to the red Witterkin, the horrific path of poison that had sliced through them like a blade. The deep, unsettling sound the scarlet Witterkin had made.

By the time she had finished, her chest heaved and her fists clenched the paper so hard it threatened to tear. She recalled the dream she'd had of the Witterkin while on Crystal Mountain, the depth of the being's peace—shattered by pain. It was easy to forget the ones who could not testify on their own behalf.

"Thank you, Nya," the middle judge said and glanced questioningly at the other judges.

Nya moistened her dry lips. "Your Honor, may I add something?"

The sheriff glared at her, but she held firm to her resolution.

The middle judge nodded and opened his hand for her to continue. Nya's eyes closed briefly. She was not charming like Goran, nor was she eloquent. Her tongue was a dull blade in her mouth. Still, she must move it to push out what she had to say. "My brother—" She cleared her throat, wetted her lips again, and plunged on. "Goran did a terrible thing, but I don't think he's entirely to blame. The people of Sundyr—myself included—have lost sight over the years of how precious the Witterkin are. Most view them now as no more than strange plants. If that misconception continues, then this *will* happen again, and when it does, the damage might not be as easy to repair." She paused, dragging in a tight breath. She wished she could explain how important the Witterkin were without having to say where she'd gotten the information. If the Keepers knew the Witterkin recorded time in the form of memories, then they must have figured out how to observe those memories somehow. What uses could such time recorders have in her world if people learned how to peer into them without inflicting damage? Could the Witterkin tell them something about their own path into the future? She had opened her mouth to continue when the judge cut in,

"Thank you, Nya."

Her eyes widened. "But I—"

"Your Honors," the sheriff said, "do you wish to question the witness?"

"I do," said the first of the three judges, a stout man with a scruffy red beard. He leaned forward and tented his fingers. "Nya, are you prone to fainting?"

She blinked, still reeling from the harsh interruption. "No, Your Honor."

"In your statement, you said that the sounds in the Witterkin cave 'climbed into your head,' so to speak, and made you pass out. Am I correct?"

"Yes, Your Honor."

"With plugged ears, I assume this would not have happened."

Nya opened her mouth and then closed it. His words had not been framed as a question.

He went on, "Both you and the Windsinger were injured during your time in the Witterkin, but Yaromir's injuries were less severe. Do you have an explanation for that?"

There it was. The question she had known would come. Her stomach clenched, but she managed to hold the judge's gaze as she shook her head.

"Very well." He unclasped his hands and sat back. "That is all."

And so it was.

The sheriff wasted no time removing her from the chamber. She was let back in hours later to be told that the contents of Goran's outbuilding would be confiscated and that because the opening in the Witterkin was now vulnerable, the strip of land it occupied would be confiscated as well. Nya was then dismissed.

Later that day, she learned that since dead people couldn't be charged for crimes, no one had been charged for the destruction of the Witterkin. Other charges were laid. Dren was found guilty of accepting a bribe from Goran. For this wilful misuse of his duty, he would be executed. As for Faina, she was both fined and sentenced to jail for her part in the abduction plot. And that was it.

Nya caught a glimpse of Yaro only once during the hearing. He looked tired but well groomed as he was escorted down a hallway toward the courtroom where he would read his witness statement. He didn't notice her as she rounded the corner, and she didn't try to catch his attention. She doubted the guards would let them converse, and what could they say to one another anyway in such a cold, uninviting space and in earshot of others?

At last, she was allowed to return home. If one could call it a home. Her servants were stiff and distant with her, even the stableman, who had never been less than courteous. The path leading to her brother's outbuilding had been taken over by watchmen. She could not keep some of her curtains open for fear they would look in while passing by. Spy on the witch.

Fortunately, she was too busy to give these problems much thought. After meeting with the lawyer to receive the deed to Goran's property, she had a list of duties to fulfill, which included visiting the tenant farmers and hearing their various excuses for why they couldn't pay their full rents. Nya knew they were toying with her, but she didn't have the energy to argue with them. She ought to hire a steward, but again, it seemed like too much trouble. And who would work for her? Yasna had had such a hard time finding help that she had taken in an old sailor. Knowing Nya's luck, such a man would filch Nya's money and vanish without a trace.

***

A week after the hearing, Nya sat in her father's old chair by the hearth, watching fire glitter through the crystal shard between her fingers. As the moments passed, her cares fell away and the mystery of her strange heritage crept over her again. She hadn't gathered herbs in weeks, not because she couldn't spare the time—she had always made time to forage—but because she feared the temptation to dive into them. In the cave, there had only been a few spiny weeds, but in the field they went on forever. She could lose herself in their twining roots. It would be a good way to disappear for a while.

Just as her fey grandmother had done.

Her brow furrowed as she recalled that strange event.

The woman's death remained a mystery—if indeed she had died at all. After her husband passed away, she had ghosted down to the harbor and stolen a boat. The night had been stormy, the waves white-tipped—an unusual occurrence in the Sundyr Harbor.

The stolen boat was spotted bobbing against Cape Strach the following afternoon, her grandmother's mangled, sodden sweater at the bottom of it. No body was ever recovered.

Nya closed her eyes and felt the cold gray water, the driving wind, the jutting black rocks. Where had the woman gone? Had she truly perished, or had her suicide at sea been a ruse? A sly bit of misdirection? Had she untied the boat, thrown her sweater into it, and let it bob away, only to sneak back home—not to the Stary Manor, but to her real home across the bridge between worlds, as she had always planned to do?

The blackened wood settled in the hearth. She pushed the crystal back into her pouch, got up, and tossed a couple of logs onto the dying fire. She stood for a few moments, staring at the shape of the logs. For some reason, they reminded her of the shadowy outline of the amorous giants on the hill.

She sank back into the chair with a sigh. She hated being alone with her thoughts. She ought to talk to someone about what had happened in the otherworld and afterward. She would have loved to confide in Yaro, but how would he react if she told him about her meeting with the Keepers? Their friendship was complicated enough without adding an additional layer of intrigue.

Yasna would gladly listen, but if Nya threw her a crumb, the older lady would want the whole cake, and Nya wasn't ready to tell her everything. Certainly not about her power. Nya wasn't even sure how Yaro felt about it. *If* she had interpreted his action in the sea cave correctly.

So many unknowns. Life before her father's death seemed simple now. Yet despite all the complications, Nya felt more herself than she had in years. There was a calmness inside her, a steadiness that had not been there before. Or, at least, it had not been for many years.

***

The next morning, she readied herself to ride to Yaro's workshop. Goran's windstone had to be made, whether or not he'd received his ceremonial burning. Since her father's stone hadn't yet been placed, she would have both stones placed at the same time.

She riffled through her wardrobe, trying on three frocks before settling on a dove gray one. But a fancy garment didn't make one passable. The mirror set in the wardrobe showed a slender, limp-haired goblin with red marks on her hands. She fished the crystal out of her pouch and watched her reflection change—limp hair grew thick and glossy, small lips gained fullness, dogteeth receded. Somehow she was still Nya, but now she was beautiful.

Her throat burned, and she shoved the shard angrily back into her pouch. She hadn't fretted about her looks before. Why now? She closed the wardrobe doors and walked away with firmness in her step.

She took the carriage into town, drawing the curtains fully across so no one would see her. As she'd suspected—and dreaded—the workshop bustled with waiting clients, a few of them relatives of those who had died as a result of Goran's plan. As Nya strode in, their chattering ceased and they shuffled away from her, as if the very air she breathed might poison them. Some probably longed to spit on her, or worse. Yaro's well-known respect for her might be the only thing keeping them in check.

The Windsinger's weary face turned toward the door, and he smiled. She had no idea how he could find a smile in the sour silence, but he did, and it made her lips twitch up. It was amazing how much more at ease she felt in his presence than the last time she had stood in this shop. The rhythmic tapping of his helper's chisel started up, lightening the tense atmosphere.

Perhaps Yaro realized he wouldn't get anywhere with his clients until she was gone, for he waved her over at once. As she stepped closer, she saw that the red welts on his face and neck were fading, but they must still cause a measure of discomfort. She looked away, pushing her lips together. She longed to make a herbal salve and run it over every one of them, but the thought felt too possessive.

"How are you, Nya?"

There was real concern in his voice. "Getting by," she said, aware of all the eyes on her. "How about you?"

"Busy." His eyes flicked to the nearby customer, who was impatiently tapping the toe of his boot. "Too busy to think or to see friends."

"Sounds familiar."

Someone cleared their throat, and Nya sighed. She said, "I came to order Goran's stone so he can add his voice to the windsong." Briefly, she told him what she needed. It wasn't much. No elaborate engravings or flourishes. Her fancy brother would have been horrified. But Goran was dead.

He'd have all the time in the world to wail about it once his stone was set on the hill.

A glint of pleasure, so fleeting she might have imagined it, touched Yaro's eyes in response. "Are you sure you want me to choose his voice *and* location?"

"Yes. I'm sure." He always knew exactly how the stones should sound and where to put them.

She turned before he could frame a response, took a step toward the door, and then paused. Her eyes widened at the small windstone that lay on the floor by his desk. The last time she had seen it, Yaro was crouched on the floor of the Witterkin cave, working the bellows. "Did you…go to the cave to retrieve that?" she almost whispered, gesturing to the stone.

"No, the sheriff did. He returned it after the hearing." He tugged on his chin. "I haven't decided where to put it yet."

An odd feeling flowed through her as she stared at the windstone. It was as if a chill wind had rushed into the workshop, startling and eerie on a warm summer's day. She met Yaro's unconcerned gaze.

His mouth tightened, and he gave a slight nod. "I'll move it today," he promised.

***

She had trouble sleeping that night. The wind slammed against her window like a battering fist. Summer was nearing its end, and the warm nights had become cool and gusty. She forced her mind to empty and gradually drifted off into a restless sleep.

A vivid dream took shape around her. She was in darkness, the bottom half of her legs lodged in some heavy, sticky mud. Wind whispered over the shadowy landscape, lifting no leaves and rustling no grass. The sound felt oddly barren. Lightning flashed then, and she gasped in shock. She was trapped in a vast sea of red muck. A standing stone jutted before her, and on it crouched one of the long-limbed Keepers. She could not tell which.

The flash faded, leaving her in pitch darkness. Nya struggled against the sickening weight of the sludge. "Merima?" she queried. When no reply came, she dragged in a harsh breath and shouted, "What do you want from me? I won't push myself on Yaro. I won't."

There came a splash and a gurgle, then silence. Another searing flash cut the sky. In that instant, she glimpsed Merima's frozen, unseeing eyes. The Keeper lay on her back in the muck, her limbs still, her rich, dark skin now mottled and corpse-pale.

Nya screamed herself awake.

She sat upright in bed, breathing hard. *Just a dream,* she told herself firmly, and then repeated the words out loud. Wind whistled through the windowpane. She got out of bed, opened the curtains, and went still, listening to the soft patter of rain. Gradually, it ceased and the wind calmed, but still she stood, every hair on her body raised.

A distant glow hung in the darkness in the direction of the mountain.

The light was too broad and vague to come from a single lamp in a tenant cottage. What was it then?

She hoped the Witterkin were safe. She hadn't ventured close to them in a while. The nearby watchmen had given her a sense of safety, but perhaps that feeling had been misguided. The men didn't keep watch over the whole length of the fence, only a narrow stretch at the base of a hill, and she had never been sure if all the conspirators had been caught.

Her jaw tightened. Something was happening. If she didn't investigate it now, tomorrow might be too late.

She lit a lamp, dressed quickly, and tiptoed down the hallway to the stairs. Her hand found her mother's carvings on the banister, and she took comfort from them. She shrugged on a warm coat and boots before slipping out the door.

The night sky was hazy with clouds, the ground wet from fresh rain. Nya edged around the manor until she faced the empty fields. She paused then, squinting in the darkness. Prickles danced up her spine. There was no doubt about it—the light hung somewhere at the foot of the mountain. What was happening?

Opting for stealth, she switched off her lamp and pushed softly through the wet grass. It would have been wiser to take the path, but she didn't want to encounter a night watchman along the way. The wet grass tugged on her boots, reminding her of a certain night spent in the other world. A dog barked as she skirted a tenant farm, and a lamp blinked on in a cottage window. She walked on, passing another farm before approaching the Witterkin. By now, the distant glow had brightened and separated into vague points of light. She knew the land well enough to pinpoint its origin to the confiscated stretch of Witterkin. What was going on there in the dead of night?

Suddenly she staggered to a stop, her breath white in the damp air. *No.* She shook her head jerkily, her hand lifting to her mouth. *It can't be.*

The silence around her deepened. Into it bled the Witterkin's scarlet cry. Her legs started moving again. A man shouted at her from somewhere, but she pushed on toward the crest of the hill. Light washed over her, so many lamps, so many men. Someone grabbed her arm, but she wrenched away, slammed him over the head with her unlit lamp, and kept running down the hill toward the cave. She didn't know what she would do, only that it had to stop. The Witterkin's pain had to end.

"Nya!" The sheriff's voice. She should have known he would be involved. Footsteps thudded behind her. She wanted to scream that the Witterkin were hurting, that memories were blinking out like stars, but her throat was swollen and painful.

The sheriff caught up with her, as she knew he would, snatched away her lamp, and shackled her. His hands weren't rough, but they weren't gentle either. She found her voice. "What are they doing? Answer me!"

The sheriff's mouth tightened. "Take her to the courthouse and let her calm down," he ordered a watchman. His hand fell on her shoulder. "This isn't what you think, Nya, and it's not the end of the world."

CHAPTER FIFTEEN

Yaro

The early-morning light fell warmly on the dining table. Yaro blinked his sleepy eyes at it and forced himself to eat what lay on his plate. He was exhausted. He'd never worked such long days before. His father used to limit the hours spent in the workshop so that the two of them would always be home in time to eat together as a family. *The dead can wait,* he used to say. But this was different. Yaro had personally killed two of these dead ones, and while he didn't regret his actions at Cape Strach, he felt responsible to their relatives in a way he had never experienced before.

It was a nightmare situation. Someone else ought to be creating the two windstones, but there was no other. He couldn't even be sure they would have the correct voices, since he was unable to separate his personal feelings from the task. He had set everything aside to finish them, knowing that the longer they sat undone, the harder he would find it to complete them.

Take an apprentice, a voice said. It was time and past time. But as always, his heart recoiled from the thought.

He finished his breakfast without tasting it and trudged out the door.

It would have been a beautiful day to visit Nya. Sunlight glistened on the rain-wetted bushes and rooftops. The air was still and slightly hazy. Clouds hung over the ocean, but they were far off yet.

There was always tomorrow, he thought. If he finished the two stones today, he would feel free to take an afternoon off.

No one waited for him at the workshop door, not even his helper, who was usually there to take his horse. Was the lad sick? He hadn't missed a day before, not even after he was beat up some weeks ago. Maybe something had held him up, and he would get here eventually.

Yaro stabled his horse and then unlocked the workshop's heavy door. "Tierney!" he called as he stepped inside. The lad had a key as well, though he rarely used it. Yaro was unsurprised by the answering silence. It would have been strange for Tierney to enter before Yaro arrived. He took a step and then halted, frozen.

The Witterkin windstone was gone.

He looked around, hoping without hope that Tierney had tucked it away somewhere. His search took him to a shelf that held an assortment of modified bellows. And of course, the smallest was missing. A sheet of paper lay in its place. The writing on it would have been illegible to anyone else, but Yaro had learned to decipher Tierney's hand. The note read, *The sheriff wanted the Witterkin stone right away and ordered me to help him with it. I'm sorry if I did wrong.*

Yaro groaned and pressed the letter to his forehead. There could only be one reason for needing that stone: damage to the Witterkin.

The poor boy. Yaro knew how much pressure the sheriff could exert. But Sheriff Neclan was a fool if he thought Tierney could heal the red Witterkin. Yaro used the bellows on windstones during their crucial finishing stage to perfect their individual "songs." Tierney had never been involved in that process. Yaro doubted the boy could even fasten the modified bellows to a windstone, much less windsing, but if the sheriff demanded it, he would exhaust himself trying.

Letting the note fall to the floor, he exited the workshop.

Unease filled him as he fetched his horse and took to the road again. While logic told him that the damage could have happened anywhere along the Witterkin ring, he strongly suspected it had occurred at the Stary's confiscated property. Was Nya aware of it?

There was no reason why she should be. And yet somehow it wouldn't surprise him.

He vividly recalled the twisting weed in the cave, which had saved both their lives. While he was still unsure of what had caused its movement, Nya's intense yet unseeing gaze made him suspect *her*. But how was she *supposed* to look with a knife at her throat and blood running down her neck? For all he knew, the weeds were but another exotic piece of magic, like the Witterkin.

Still, she had always possessed an affinity for green things, and especially for the Witterkin. If they were suffering, she probably knew it.

But if she didn't know…

He looked down, twisting the reins around his palm. If she didn't, then she should. He would stop at her home first and tell her what happened. He grimaced at the thought. She had been right to be nervous about where he had left the Witterkin's windstone. He had meant to move it yesterday, but he'd been so tired that he hadn't remembered until he was abed. What would she think of him now?

They badly needed to talk, to *really* talk—if such a thing were even possible.

He passed the well-trampled road to Goran's old property and pushed on to the Stary manor. The stableman appeared, glared at him, and strode away. The man must still believe that Yaro had hurt Nya. Heaving a sigh, he left his horse in the drive, mounted the short stair, and pounded the knocker. The door opened, and the maid appeared.

"Nya's gone, Master Yaro," the girl said before he could open his mouth. She leaned out the door and glanced around. "I don't right know where she is."

"You didn't see her this morning?"

"Nobody's seen her. She must have gone out in the middle of the night." She leaned back in, and her voice grew muffled. "Her coat and boots are missing..."

Yaro didn't wait to hear the rest but mounted his horse again and rode off down the road. He meant to ride up the path that led to Goran's unfinished manor, but when he was still a dozen yards away, two riders came to a halt at the mouth of the path and waited for him.

One was Sheriff Neclan. The crafty man greeted him with an overly warm smile.

Yaro did not return it. "Where is Nya? Is she by the cave?"

"No, she is not."

Something in his voice made Yaro suspicious. "But she *was* there, wasn't she?" Yaro dismounted and approached him. The second rider—a watchman—fingered his weapons, but at a glance from the sheriff, his hands fell to his sides. Yaro said, "You took a windstone and bellows from my workshop today. Why? What happened?"

The sheriff hesitated and then shrugged. "We had to kill a few Witterkin to remove the bodies in the cave."

"Of course you did," Yaro replied acidly. "And now the neighboring Witterkin have turned scarlet."

"The damage can be repaired, as you well know."

"Where is Nya?"

"She trespassed and attacked an officer last night. She is being held in the courthouse." As he spoke, another watchman cantered toward him up the path. The sheriff conferred with him in hushed tones, then turned back to Yaro and said in a commanding voice, "You must come with me."

"No." Yaro shook his head roughly. "I won't help you fix this. You broke the law when you disturbed the Witterkin, the very law you were supposed to uphold!"

"That law was amended two days ago."

Yaro's eyes widened. "After everything that happened?" When the sheriff didn't respond, his shock changed to anger. "But you made sure to take Nya's land first! Don't tell me that cave won't be mined after this."

"I don't make the laws, I just uphold them."

"That's good, because there's no law that says I can be forced to windsing." He wheeled away and mounted his horse.

"You will!" the sheriff shouted. He made a gesture, and the two watchmen drew their bows.

"Kill me," Yaro prompted them.

After a tight silence, the sheriff had his men lower their bows. Neclan spoke to the ground as he approached Yaro, his horse flattening its ears at the sheriff's hesitancy. "What do you want? Nya?"

"That's a start. Release her from the courthouse and bring her here."

At once, he ordered one of his men to fetch her. "Anything more?" he asked dryly.

"Yes. I want you to send Tierney home. Now."

Nya

Nya stood panting against the wall of her prison cell, a ruined mattress on the floor by her feet and torn bedding strewn everywhere. She couldn't remember a time when she had been this angry. She clenched and unclenched her fists against her thighs, trying to get control of herself, but her thoughts kept feeding her rage. She had trusted the sheriff to protect the Witterkin. Instead, he had poisoned them while she slept. And now what could be done?

She drew a long breath and let it out slowly. *Think.* The sheriff wouldn't want the red Witterkin to spread either, so he would have to fetch Yaro to heal them. Perhaps he meant to use Nya against Yaro as leverage. Once the Witterkin were healed, would he try to silence her and Yaro somehow, so they couldn't incriminate him?

The thought had scarcely grazed her mind when a door clanged and footsteps sounded in the hallway. Nya seized the mangled straw mattress, rolled it up, and held it like a weapon in front of her.

The young guard halted at her cell door and stared at her with wide eyes. "Ah…the sheriff wants you."

"The last time a guard came to my cell and said that, I ended up being drugged and abducted."

"Well, it's different this time."

She noticed with satisfaction that his hand trembled as he unlocked the door. He stood aside, his eyes on the flagstones.

"Where *is* the sheriff?" she asked.

"Back at your property, with Yaromir. The Windsinger asked for you."

Nya tossed aside the mattress and hurried to the door. "Does Yaro have a heavy pack with him?"

"I didn't see one."

"Never mind. Let's go."

Despite Nya's protestations, the guard made her ride in a carriage rather than on horseback. Wings wouldn't have been fast enough. Nya clutched the seat with both hands as the carriage plodded along, her thoughts racing.

Yaro didn't need her in order to windsing, so why had he demanded her presence?

What if he hadn't? she thought suddenly. Dizzily.

After Yaro did his work, the sheriff would want no loose ends. No witnesses to his atrocity. The solution would be to bring Nya and Yaro together in one place—a secluded place—where they could both be disposed of. Silenced.

She leaned back in the seat and forced her jaw to unclench. She hoped she was wrong, but she didn't know Neclan well enough to be sure what he was capable of.

The carriage arrived at the path leading to Goran's unfinished outbuildings. A watchman standing in the road said a few words to the guard, then the horses turned and the ride became bumpier. It finally halted at the outbuilding, and the guard disembarked. Nya stepped out before he could offer her his hand. "Did Yaro give a reason for wanting me here?"

"No."

The answer didn't relieve her mounting anxiety, and she had no choice but to follow him toward the slope. The Witterkin's haunting cry pierced her as they neared the fence. She glanced sideways at the guard. "What happened to the Witterkin?"

There was a long pause before he shrugged and said, "We had to kill some along the path and in the cave to remove the bodies. Somehow, the redness spread."

Nya shook her head but said nothing. She didn't believe that the sheriff would break a law to remove three rotten corpses. But the guard wasn't about to tell her the truth, even if he was cognizant of it.

The scene at the base of the hill was as she expected. Yaro and the sheriff waited by the scarlet mouth of the path, Yaro's arms folded and his chin lifted defiantly, the sheriff facing away from him, tapping his booted foot. Several men stood on watch duty nearby, their faces averted from the mass of red Witterkin. There was no sign of the corpses—a fact that relieved her more than she cared to admit.

Anger drained from Yaro's face when he saw her coming toward him. His gaze flicked to a torn cuff on her arm. "Are you all right?"

A dry smile tugged on her lips. "I'm fine. I did this to myself. Yaro, did you ask for me, or—"

"I did." He pressed his lips together, then leaned closer. "I thought you ought to be here, not rotting in a cell. Did I do wrong?"

Before she could reply, the sheriff cut in, "Is she coming into the cave with us?"

"No," Yaro replied, predictable as ever. But to Nya's surprise, he added, "I'm not doing this in the cave. I don't think I'll need to."

At his request, the Witterkin windstone and bellows were hauled from the cave to the mouth of the path. Yaro moved them to a place just inside the mouth and set them up. Meanwhile, the sheriff handed Nya a pair of beeswax earplugs. "So you won't pass out," he said.

Several watchmen had already inserted their own into their ears. Nya's lips compressed as she stared at the small objects on her palm. The judge's comment about plugging one's ears to prevent fainting while in the cave came back to her, and she knew with a sick certainty that the Witterkin's poisoning had been planned even before the court hearing. They had confiscated her property, not to protect the Witterkin in the cave, but to destroy them so gold could be mined.

"I'll take them too," Yaro muttered.

The sheriff said, "Don't you need to hear in order to—?"

"No. Besides, doubtless I'll still hear something."

Yaro plugged his ears and then looked at Nya until she inserted her own.

The world went quiet. She folded her arms and shivered, though it wasn't cold. Yaro's arms began moving as he worked the strange bellows. Nya shifted closer to him, wanting to be near if something went wrong. He didn't seem to notice the movement; all his mental energy was focused on the task.

Time plodded by, and little by little, the red faded and a muddy shade of green took over. Still, Yaro pressed on, doubtless hoping that his playing would fully restore the color, but it was not to be. At last, he removed his plugs and stood up, gaze sweeping the green mass.

Nya yanked out her own and listened. The sound was almost right, but a hint of desperation clung to it, like that of someone beaten one too many times. She glanced at the sheriff and was stunned to find him looking unconcerned. Perhaps he judged it didn't matter what shade they were or how they sounded, as long as they stopped expanding.

He views them as mere plants, she thought. And with that realization, another followed: this poisoning would happen again, not in some distant future, but within her lifetime. And one day, the damage inflicted would be too great for a Windsinger to heal, and all the Witterkin would have to be destroyed. Such a tragedy might be possible in this world, if the authorities obtained enough poison, but what would happen in the other, where such poison didn't exist? The Witterkin spanned both worlds. Damage that happened on one side spread into the other. And kept spreading.

Do you understand? she had been asked on Crystal Mountain.

"Yes," Nya whispered, her breathing deepening. *If you won't protect them, then you won't have them.*

Yaro had turned to speak to the sheriff. No one watched Nya as she inched the toe of her boot into one of the Witterkin. A sensation akin to sparks shot through her. But she barely felt it, for the moment the contact was made, she plunged her awareness into the crackling green depths.

Immediately, she felt a blinding shock, as if a falling boulder had struck her. She reeled at the impact, managing to retain consciousness by a thread. She resisted the urge to retreat back into her body. Gradually, the shock wore off, and she relaxed a little. The bright core of the being edged away from her like a nervous animal. She wanted—no, *needed*—to commune with it, and share its senses. She thought about what she'd sensed from the greenshifter when he'd explored her. Each vine had been part of him, an extension of his mind. She refined her focus and then expanded, sending tendrils of herself out. The being she had entered clasped them with its own.

An astonishing world opened to her, one she had merely glimpsed in a dream while on Crystal Mountain. The Witterkin's core hung like a bright star in a vast universe of gathered memories, each one connected through fine threads of awareness. But this strange landscape didn't obscure the being's perception of the world outside it. Unlike in the cave weeds, Nya could clearly hear and see everything, even her own upright body.

And it saw even more than humans did.

A long, shimmering cord hung around the foot of the mountain. The other world lay beyond it—a rippling, underwater vision of purple fields and far-off crags.

Nya had found the bridge between worlds. The Witterkin straddled it, some on one side and some on the other.

The sheriff's words drifted over. She sensed the Witterkin recording them as sounds without understanding their meaning. Could she make herself be understood?

Danger, she warned the being.

More tendrils caught at her, and she sensed the being's attention.

Memory was key. Nya conjured up memories of the blackened path through the Witterkin, the scent of poison in the air; *danger*. She thrust out an image of retreating vines, then one of a peaceful field of purple flowers filled with clumps of healthy Witterkin. *Safety. Peace.* Then the vines again. *Move.* She pushed out the feelings with the words. Again and again, with increasing urgency.

Nothing happened. The being seemed mesmerized, as though it watched an unfolding dream. Nya gave up finally and rested. But the being continued to focus on her. There was an odd stillness in it, like the gathering calm before a storm. Then it abruptly pulled its tendrils away from her, severing Nya's vision of the outside world. As its attention shifted from Nya, filaments between memories flashed and crackled. Nya shrank her presence to a small point in order to avoid the painful sensation they roused, and then smaller still. At last, with an inward scream, she fled back to her body.

"...standing too close!" a voice snapped. Hands gripped her shoulders, and she was jerked back. The world spun dizzyingly.

"Nya?" Yaro's voice, filled with concern.

She drew the Windsinger's hands off her shoulders and shifted so they were face to face. "I'm fine."

He shook his head and had opened his mouth to speak when something over her shoulder made him gasp and draw away. Nya turned, still dizzy, and froze in shock.

The Witterkin were moving toward the mountain. Not a few at first, as she had expected, but all of them at once, like a great swath of ocean weed drawn in by the tide. Unencumbered by roots, the green mass glided over and between rocks as it made its way across the bridge between worlds (now invisible to her eyes).

"Where are they going?" the sheriff shouted behind her.

No one answered him. No one moved. It was like watching an eclipse of the sun, but one in which no light returned.

After a while, the mass thinned. From a distance, it appeared to be compressing, but Nya knew the truth: the Witterkin were passing into the other world.

No. It was happening too fast. They couldn't just leave in a day. In an hour. Her throat burned. Her hungry eyes followed them, wanting these last moments to be seared in her memory forever.

And then they were gone, leaving her standing in a barren strip of gray rock.

Tears streaked her cheeks. She had loved the Witterkin. And now they were gone from her forever.

Yaro's hands fell lightly on her shoulders again. "Are you all right?"

The question seemed unimportant, even irrelevant. "Wonder is gone from the world," she whispered. "How can anyone be all right?"

CHAPTER SIXTEEN

Nya, Yaro, the sheriff, and two of the watchmen made their way back to the path in stunned silence.

The fence seemed a foolish, flimsy thing now that the Witterkin it had once protected were gone. And really, truly gone. Nya could see no hint of them even when squinting into the distance. They had huddled by the mountain for countless generations, their high-pitched sound as constant as the air, as the sea. Its absence was more than painful—it was shocking. And yet she could not regret her decision to urge them away. A part of her wished she could have joined them.

Too late now. All she had left of that world was the crystal shard and a few crumpled plants.

And myself, she thought, for some of her blood must have come from that place, likely from her grandmother.

The men mounted their horses at Goran's outbuilding and waited while Nya climbed into the carriage; then, as one, they continued on.

The group wasn't far from the main road when Yaro nudged his horse past the others until he was almost alongside the sheriff. Nya strained to hear his words amid the clopping of hooves. She grasped enough to be surprised and a little touched.

He demanded that Nya's land be returned to her or that she be compensated. If not, he would take the matter to the King's High Court. After a long pause, the sheriff replied, his words too low for Nya to make out, but Yaro seemed content with what was said; the set of his shoulders relaxed, and he fell back into his place in line. She wondered what had compelled him to take such an immense gamble. If the sheriff hadn't agreed to resolve the matter, Yaro would've been forced to carry out his threat or risk losing his honor.

She was still pondering the peculiarity when a familiar buggy pulled up by the mouth of the path.

Yasna.

Nya's hands clenched the carriage seat. Suddenly, she wanted her friend very badly.

Yaro hung back after Nya disembarked from the carriage. He fidgeted with the reins, his earlier tension still hanging on him. "Can we speak later?" he asked.

"Of course. Come by whenever you like."

Satisfied, he bade her farewell and trotted away, leaving Nya and Yasna alone on the road.

The older lady stepped down from her buggy and approached her. "What happened?"

Nya's mouth opened and then closed. How could she tell her the Witterkin were gone? Pain swelled in her chest. She folded her arms against it and stared at the ground. "I—"

"Come here, Nitty." Nya looked up to find Yasna's arms flung wide.

Nya fled into them. Tears broke out of her at last. She wept for the Witterkin, for her brother's death, for everything she had been holding in, unable to release. She had not been hugged by anyone this way in years.

Yasna drew a little away from her with a gentle smile. "Will you tell me everything now?"

"I guess." Nya wiped her eyes. She smelled like Yasna's almond oil. "You know, you've become like a mother to me."

Yasna's light hold on her forearms tightened. "I could be that for you if you want me to be."

A nervous laugh broke out of Nya. "You won't want to be after you hear my story."

"Try me. You might be surprised."

"All right. But at your house, not mine."

The choice of location turned out to be a good one. Yasna's servant was in town doing errands, leaving the house empty of prying ears.

Nya was true to her word: she gave Yasna everything, and the older lady listened, sipping her tea with a steady hand until the end, when she learned that the Witterkin were gone. Her cup slammed down on the saucer, and she stared at Nya without comprehension. "All of them? It can't be."

After Nya assured her that it was, Yasna declared that she would have to see it for herself. She grew restless after that, her looks full of rueful impatience. Nya took the hint and made up a reasonable excuse for leaving. Yasna brought her back home and then headed up the path toward the Witterkin. Nya watched her from afar, feeling slightly guilty for not offering to come with her, but if her friend had wanted company, she would have asked for it.

Nya wandered her house as the light fell, restless yet weary.

She flinched when a knock fell on the door. Was it Yasna, she thought, or Yaro? She reached it before the maid and flung it open.

A red-haired woman from town stood on the porch. She spoke in a hurried whisper. "Nya, I'd like some hillwort if you have it."

Nya grinned as she regarded her customer. "I do have some. Come in for a few moments. I'll have the maid bring tea."

***

Early the next morning, Nya went into her herb shed. As always, she paused at the entrance and drank in a breath of dried plants, searching for a hint of mildew. Finding none, she did a quick inventory of her stock. She was running low on a couple of popular herbs. Today, she would have to remedy that.

She upended her pouch on the workbench and counted the various seeds from the purple and yellow plants she had gathered in the otherworld. Despite the battering they had suffered, most were still intact. They would hopefully grow, and no one would know where they'd come from. She planted them carefully in whatever spare pots she could find, then rinsed her hands in a bucket and left.

It was a beautiful late summer day. A turquoise sky peeked between threads of wispy clouds; bees drifted from flower to flower. Her feet took her toward the mountain, because the herbs she needed always grew best in its shadow. Unfortunately, that meant venturing close to the Witterkin fence. She snapped off a piece of grass and chewed one end. Once the local landowners learned that the Witterkin were gone, they would waste no time removing the fence and hacking into the mountain in search of gold.

But others would mourn the loss. The Witterkin had drawn visitors from all over the world. Sundyr still had Cemetery Hill, with its unique singing stones, but without the Witterkin, she doubted people would make the effort to come. A merchant had once told her that to the outside world, Sundyr and Witterkin were synonymous. How would the little town be viewed now?

Her head was lowered, her eyes resolutely on the ground when a familiar voice, raised in greeting, made her heart turn over in her chest. She turned.

And there was Yaro, long legs pushing through the field grass as he approached her. He wore a plain unbelted jerkin over a loose shirt and dark hose. The wind had had its way with his hair, which was still a bit powdered by stone dust.

The blade of grass fell, and a slow smile curved her lips. The dread she had once felt around him was gone. Doubtless, the shadow of her mother's death would rear its head between them again, but when it did, she suspected she could push through it.

He slowed when he was still some feet away. "The maid said you were out here. Are you collecting herbs?"

"I was. Now I'm talking to you."

He grinned and looked down.

Nya went on, "I didn't think you'd come by today. You seemed busy when I stopped by your workshop."

"I am. But we need to talk." Then, as if to belie his words, he fell silent.

Nya walked to the fence, and they stood together for a time, just looking at the barren strip.

"Where do you think they went?" he asked.

"To another world."

He glanced at her. "You really believe that?"

"Yes."

She thought he would ask her why. Instead, he closed his eyes and drew in a long breath. Wind stirred his dark hair. "Close your eyes, Nya, and listen."

"For what?" she said, but he didn't answer. She shut her eyes and heard wind. Wind in the long grass behind her, wind in the craggy foot of the mountain. It was a gentle sound. Endless. Yaro's voice seeped into it,

"There's still wonder in *this* world, if you know where to find it."

She remembered her windstone, wailing in the cave, and nodded. Yes, there was. The thought eased something inside her.

Her eyes opened, and she looked at him. It occurred to her that it didn't matter now whether she married him or not. That fact should have made her feel relieved, but it had the opposite effect. A rope that had bound them was gone. She wanted it back.

He had wanted to talk. She searched for something to say. "Thanks, for getting me out of prison yesterday, and for taking a stand about my property."

He grimaced. "You overheard my conversation with the sheriff."

"Part of it."

"I'm sorry about that. I was riled up over the whole thing and not thinking clearly. I should have talked to you first, before..."

She shrugged. "I said thank you, so I'm not upset. Truth be told, I'm glad someone cared enough to make a stink about it."

"I dislike it when people trample on you."

"Well, that makes two of us." She chuckled. "You seem to make the sheriff nervous."

"I have trouble controlling my temper around him."

"You have a temper?" They shared an amused smile, then he went back to gazing pensively at the space that once held Witterkin.

Nya recognized the shape of his brooding silence. He wished to say something—or perhaps to ask her a question—but was too nervous to do so. Perhaps he worried about how she would react, or worse, was afraid of the answer she would give him. She sorted through their recent encounters, wondering what might be on his mind, and gave up. She had a question of her own, and if it led to his, then so be it.

"Yaro, what do you remember…from being in the Witterkin?"

"Nothing. Just a long, muddled nightmare. What about you?"

She loosed a breathy chuckle. "One long nightmare sums it up well."

He nodded absently, and after a pause, cast her a darting glance. "Did you—have anything to do with the Witterkin leaving?"

And there it was. The question.

For an instant, she actually considered lying. They were circling one another again, inching closer in a tentative, uncertain way. But the true depth of Nya's strangeness might be enough to disturb that dance. Especially if he *hadn't* connected her with the crawling weed in the cave, as she had assumed.

She dragged a hand over her face. If she had learned anything from Goran and Faina, it was that deception was no basis for a sound relationship. "Yes. I gave them a nudge toward safety. How did you guess?"

"You looked dazed, and yet…oddly focused, just before they started moving. It reminded me of your expression in the cave when the plant…did that thing." Another question hung in his eyes.

"That was me too," she admitted. "And I don't know what to say about that. I didn't know I could do it until I was abducted. And then—I think the powerful voice of the windstone stirred something inside me, an ability that was always there but not developed yet." She glanced at him nervously, but he seemed reflective rather than upset. She leaned away from the fence and began to walk. "And what about you, Warrior Yaro? When did you have armor made and learn to use weapons?"

So he talked, and it became easy just to walk and listen. To hear him speak of his family, his past, the recent business that had swallowed his time. And gradually, it occurred to her that he wasn't bothered by her strange abilities or even surprised by her confession.

The realization startled and warmed her.

They paused again at the Witterkin fence. Nya swallowed back a sudden thickness in her throat and tried to focus on the conversation. "Sounds like you're in a difficult situation now."

He shrugged. "It'll pass, and things will return to normal."

"No doubt. Until tragedy strikes and you have another pile of stones to do. Have you ever thought seriously about taking on an apprentice?"

"Of course. That would make everything so much easier."

"Then…?"

He sighed. "To be honest, it feels wrong. Wrong in a way I can't explain. It's not something anyone in my family has ever done before. They've always had sons or daughters to train. But then I came along and…" He chuckled and clasped his hands behind his head. "No one wants to marry this ugly mug."

Nya winced. He had spoken about himself this way before, though she had never understood it. No part of him could be called ugly, or even plain. He was, very simply, beautiful. She was about to tell him so when a glitter of light peeking from his sleeve made her catch her breath.

"What's that?" she asked, pointing to a half-hidden object on the inside of his wrist.

He dropped his arms, pulled back a sleeve, and offered her his turned-up wrist. "This?"

Nya couldn't find the breath to answer. Now that she regarded the object more closely, she saw the unmistakable curling of light deep within its core. It was a polished shard from Crystal Mountain, bored through twice somehow and clasped to the inside of his wrist by a leather band.

When she didn't reply, he went on, "My mother gave it to me long ago." He glanced up at her. "And here's something strange: your grandmother gave it to *her*—the one who was pulled from the Witterkin. She said it was for me and that I should wear it always. My mom—she believed the stories about your Nan and insisted I wear it. I still remember when she gave it to me. I was only a boy, and I hated it." He ran his finger over the crystal. "It comes with a riddle of sorts. I can't recall the exact words anymore, but the gist of it is that the person who asks for it will never have seen my face." He snorted. "What nonsense. My mother probably made it up to keep me from giving it away."

Nya held out her hand. Her voice was hoarse as she asked, "C-can I...?"

He nodded and untied the band. But she didn't look at the crystal as he placed it in her palm. Her eyes were on his face, which had transformed the moment he removed the crystal. His eyes drew close together, his nose became a small lump in the middle of his face, his chin rounded and thinned, and he gained an underbite. She swallowed and pretended to study the crystal.

Words spoken, looks exchanged, all came together and made sense as the reality hit her. *Pa used to say that you two were like peas in a pod,* Goran had said. Peas indeed. All these years, she had seen beauty while others had seen ugliness. She forced her eyes up again. This was his true face, the one that looked back at him in every mirror. The other had been nought but a screen, an image glimpsed through crystal.

"What is it?" he asked. "What are you thinking?"

She cleared her throat and tried to speak. Nothing came out. After a long silence, she gasped and looked down. "Oh no, I dropped it."

"The crystal?" He knelt down and began searching the long grass. Nya joined him.

He said, "It's so small that we'll probably see the band first. Too bad it's not sunny now. That crystal reflects light like nothing I've ever seen."

Grass rustled as they both searched. And searched.

"I think it's gone," she mumbled after some minutes, and he sat up so swiftly that he banged her head.

"Sorry!" He grasped her face, as if to steady her, but his hands didn't come away.

Neither of them spoke or moved. Nya saw only his warm hazel eyes, solemn, questioning. Familiar, despite the changes he had undergone.

The moments passed, and somehow they entered another place, one warmer, closer. The intensity that sometimes gathered in his eyes was there again; it seemed to fill the air between them with a charged sort of heaviness. It was Yaro. It would always be Yaro. The wonder of him swept through her. She could lose herself in it, dive down into his roots and try to find the source of him.

She closed her eyes, and he kissed her—a slow, lingering kiss that she never wanted to end.

She thought of the crystal she had slipped into her pocket. She might give it back. Or she might not. The choice was hers.

Yaro broke the kiss and cupped her face, speechless, it seemed.

"I have a story to tell you," she said before he could find words. She grinned. Probably a gobliny grin. A child would run from it. Yaro remained fixed in place, his thumb stirring the hairs at her temple.

Suddenly she got to her feet and opened her arms to the beautiful day. It was time to talk. "So listen up, Windsinger!"

BOOKS BY WK GREYLING

THE AURE DUOLOGY

**Beneath the Roots*

**White Bird*

THE MOTHERTREE DUOLOGY

**Silver Light*

**Battle for the Woodlands*

ABOUT THE AUTHOR

Canadian novelist W.K. Greyling lives in the maritime province of Nova Scotia. When she's not writing, she spends her time curating the music library for Ancient FM, an online medieval and Renaissance radio station.

Printed in Great Britain
by Amazon